Brake, Rattle and Roll

The plan is not only to brake, but to avoid being rear-ended by stray enemy ships that pass through, while avoiding enemy fire the whole time. To do this, Emerald has ordered a very stressful maneuver called a controlled tumble, much like its counterpart performed in atmosphere.

"Initiate sequence. Fire attitude rockets. Reverse thrust engines activated. Ten. Nine, eight. Power at seventy-eight percent. Four, three, two, one. Fire."

The sudden jolt which follows the wild spin knocks bodies into restraining straps with bone-snapping suddenness.

Emerald monitors her output, fighting the bucking ship and the pain in her joints.

"We're rocking tonight," she shouts, as she sees her entire complement of ships dropping behind the enemy.

The enemy is soon to be. . . .

CUT BY EMERALD

The Combat Command Books from Ace:

COMBAT COMMAND

IN THE WORLD OF

PIERS ANTHONY'S
BIO OF A SPACE TYRANT

CUT BY EMERALD
BY
DANA KRAMER

WITH AN INTRODUCTION BY
PIERS ANTHONY

ACE BOOKS, NEW YORK

This book is an Ace original edition,
and has never been previously published.

CUT BY EMERALD

An Ace Book / published by arrangement with
Bill Fawcett & Associates

PRINTING HISTORY
Ace edition / August 1987

INTRODUCTION
by Piers Anthony

This is a game book based on my science fiction series, Bio of a Space Tyrant. If you have read one or more of these novels, it should help you, because you will understand the basic situation. However, you can still play the game if you have never heard of me or this series, because the rules will be explained to you in this volume. If you are impatient to get started, you can skip this introduction and get on with it. After all, you came here for wild adventure, not a dull essay.

But for those of you who are tolerant of essays, I have some background on the background. That is, the background of this game is my Space Tyrant series, but the series itself had its own background, which most of the readers of the novels don't know about. If you understand about this double background, it just might help you to make better decisions in the game. The person who made up the game probably hasn't bothered to read this essay, so you might even be able to outsmart her because you know something she doesn't. On the other hand, you might mess up even worse; I'm not making any promises here.

The project started when I went to the publisher and proposed to do a space opera series. Now, space opera is not an opera played in space, though a writer named Jack Vance once wrote a novel about that, entitled *Space Opera*. Rather, it is old-fashioned science fiction, just the way that Sword & Sorcery is old-fashioned fantasy. Space opera used to be full of fantastic adventure and spot lectures in science. It was a lot like horse opera, with the hero riding a spaceship instead of a horse, and blazing away with his blaster instead of a six-gun. As you might guess, a lot of it was pretty awful stuff. But I said to the publisher, with that modesty for which genre writers are known, "Suppose someone who really can write tries it?" Evidently I fooled the publisher, because I got a big contract for a series of five novels. The series has had terrible reviews and excellent sales, which is the way such things go; the reviewers never caught on to what you will learn here, but the readers had better judgment.

You may be used to fantasy, where you can use magic to do all sorts of things. I understand about that; I have been known to dabble in fantasy myself. But this is science fiction; here there is no magic, only science. However, it is advanced science, which may seem almost like magic at times. You have to understand its nature, or you will come to grief, just as you would today if you stuck your tongue in a lightbulb socket and turned on the power. Actually, that's not the best policy in this game, either; only dim bulbs do that. Maybe you stand by your right to stick your tongue anywhere you want, but it is better to keep a civil tongue in your head. If you understand the nature of electricity, you can use it to your advantage, and the same is true with the science here.

The setting is our Solar System, exactly as it is now. The time is about seven hundred years from now, and mankind has spread through the system, relieving the pressure of population expansion on Earth. All the planets have been colonized except Pluto, and most of the moons are inhabited, as well as a number of the planetoids in the Asteroid Belt. This has been accomplished by a single major scientific breakthrough: gravity shielding. Special lenses focus the streams of gravitons, which are the particles that convey the force of gravity. Think of it as you would light: you can use a magnifying glass to focus it to the burning point in a small area, while the region around that focus is shadowed. When gravity is similarly focused at the surface of a moon, it brings up the effective gravity to the level of what we feel at the surface of the Earth, one gee. Thus it is possible to build cities on Luna, Earth's moon, that have standard earth gravity, while the regions around them have even less than before. Since the cities are domed, to maintain the type and pressure of Earth's atmosphere, what's outside doesn't make much difference; the average person doesn't go out there.

The big planets pose another problem. They have too much gravity. But the same lenses handle this, too. Remember that depleted region around the gee focus? That is used to put a region in low gee, bringing it down to Earth norm. Ah, but even so there is a small problem: the four "gas giant" planets—Jupiter, Saturn, Uranus, and Neptune—don't have solid surfaces; their monstrous atmospheres simply keep compressing until they become metallic, and the pressure is thousands of bars. One bar is the pressure of the atmosphere of Earth's surface, and it really wouldn't be comfortable at a thousand bars, or even at only five or six bars. Their atmosphere isn't exactly what you'd care to breathe, either; there is almost no oxygen, and hardly any water vapor. So you can't just set up shop on Jupiter's surface.

However, the gee-shields solve this problem, too. First you put your city in a bubble—that is, a sphere that holds an Earth-type atmosphere at one bar. Then you *float* that city-bubble in the atmosphere where the pressure isn't too high, using gee-shielding to make it light enough. Because the gee-shield cuts off most of the effect of gravity, you need to spin the bubble to get your gee back by centrifugal force. Thus you are really standing horizontally inside a spinning bubble that is floating in the atmosphere of a gas giant. But to you it seems like normal ground and normal gravity, as long as you don't go too close to the center, where you might float, or try to jump too far, because you would seem to fall in a curve. This is because of the dynamics of a spinning habitat; even some well-respected hard-science writers don't seem to understand it. It can be downright dangerous to throw things, because the seeming curve could make you hit the wrong target. Remember that, when you're in the game; your life may depend on it!

So there are domes with gee-enhancement on the moons and small planets, and spinning bubbles floating around the big planets, and spinning bubbles in space. You might think this makes the Solar System crowded, but that is not the case; the space around the Sun is vast, and the different planets are light-minutes or even light-hours apart. That means you can't just pick up the phone and call your grandma on Neptune; you'd have to wait eight hours or more for her response, even with light speed transmission. If you receive a call from another planet, and there is no delay in transmission as you talk, beware; it is a faked-up call, probably by someone who means you no good. Think paranoid; that, too, may save your life.

But how do you travel? Chemical fuel is expensive, and gravity wells are deep. Well, you use the gee-shields here, too. You shield your spaceship from gravity, so that only its inertia has to be overcome. You can picture this by remembering the last time you were in a car that stalled. Did you get out and heave it onto your shoulders and carry it to the nearest service station? No, you simply pushed it along the highway. It was still a job, but a manageable one; all you had to overcome was its inertia, not its weight. A gee-shielded spaceship doesn't have to be lifted off a planet; it can simply be pushed. This makes interplanetary travel much easier. That doesn't mean that spaceships don't have engines; they use contra-terrene iron for propulsion, because iron can be handled magnetically. You wouldn't want to touch CT iron; your hand would immediately explode, its substance converting totally to energy. CT, or SeeTee, looks and acts exactly like normal matter, except for that one problem; be careful what you touch!

It is possible to travel in space without any propulsive engine, simply by shielding your little bubble-ship from the gee of one planet, while leaving it open to the gee of another. This is slow, but it works well enough when you are trying to travel from one of Jupiter's moons, such as Callisto, to Jupiter itself. This is analogous to sailboating, with gravity being the wind. Many poor people do travel that way, and you may too, when you're broke. Unfortunately there are many pirates abroad in the Jupiter ecliptic—that is, the plane of Jupiter's many moons—and they prey on such little bubbles, so most sail-bubbles never make it to their destination. About the only things the pirates respect are the guns of military vessels, and the mysterious QYV, whose couriers can be identified by marks in private regions of their bodies.

And this is the key to the real nature of this series. This entire situation is borrowed from the world of today, in perfect space-opera fashion, by no coincidence. Every planet and moon is analogous to a land mass of contemporary Earth. The planet Jupiter is the same as America, with the United States of Jupiter (the US of J) in the north, and Latin nations in the south. The moons equate to islands, such as Cuba and Hispaniola. Saturn is Asia, with the Union of Saturnine Republics (USR) in the north, and the People's Republic of Saturn, otherwise known as the Middle Kingdom, in the south. Uranus is Europe, and Neptune is Australia.

The politics of today's world are also reflected. Jupiter and Saturn have a cold war going. Indeed, the planets were colonized by the nations they resemble, and the people carried their cultures and rivalries out to the new worlds. North Jupiter hates Jupiter's moon Ganymede, whose revolutionary government turned communist and sought support from Saturn. Another moon (island), Callisto, is divided into two Hispanic nations. Of these two, Halfcal is very poor, with a corrupt government; its people take to space in unpowered bubbles, trying to reach the promised land of Jupiter, where it is supposed that everyone is rich. Actually Jupiter is sick of these Bubble People, and is apt to tow them back out to space again. This was the starting point of the Space Tyrant series. The first novel, *Refugee,* is based on the plight of the Vietnamese Boat People and the Haitian Boat People, who took to sea and were savaged by pirates, their men killed, their women raped, and their children abducted into slavery while the world ignored them. The second novel, *Mercenary,* took the U.S. military establishment as I experienced it, exaggerated the details, and translated it to space in similar fashion. The third, *Politician,* drew on the internal political situation of America. So if you have trouble keeping track of all the planets and moons and nations, just keep today's world in mind, and it should make more sense.

This is the situation into which you are about to trust your innocent little life. I'm glad it's you going there, and not me!

—Piers Anthony

Solar Geography for Bio of a Space Tyrant

Celestial Body	Earth equivalent	Known for
Mercury	South Africa	Gems
Venus	North Africa	Iron
Earth	India	
Luna	Ceylon	
Mars	Asia Minor (Moslem)	Iron (Oil)
Asteroid Belt	Pacific Islands	
	Carolines	Pornography
	Fiji	Smuggling
	Marianas	Slavery
	Samoa	Drugs
	Society	Fencing
	Solomons	Gambling
Hidalgo	Hawaii	
Chiron	Cyprus	
Jupiter North	North America (states named for popular names)	
South	South America	
Red Spot	Mexico	
Amalthea	Bahamas	
Io	Puerto Rico	
Europa	Jamaica	
Ganymede	Cuba	
Callisto	Hispaniola	
Halfcal	Haiti	
Dominant Republic	Dominican Republic	
Outer Moons	Lesser Antilles	
Saturn North	Russia	
South	China	
Inner Satellites	Philippines	
Outer Satellites	Indonesia	
Rings	Taiwan	
	Hong Kong	
Titan	Japan	
Uranus	Europe	
Miranda	Crete	
Ariel	Sardinia	
Umbriel	Ireland	
Titania	England	
Oberon	Iceland	
Neptune	Australia	
Triton	New Zealand	
Nereid	Tasmania	
Pluto	Antarctica	
Charon		

INTRODUCTION
by Bill Fawcett

You are in command. With a blare of trumpets punctuated by a hurriedly barked order, it's off to battle. Following behind are ships full of your men, trained spacemen whose lives depend upon the decisions you are about to make.

The Combat Command series puts you at the head of science fiction's toughest soldiers. In this book you are Emerald, in command of the fleet sent by Hope Hubris to flank the Marianas pirates in the climactic battle of volume two of Bio of a Space Tyrant, *Mercenary*.

Combat Command books provide one more chance to read about a favorite science fiction world and its familiar characters. These books are also a game. In each section of this game/book a military decision is described. You are given the same information as you would actually receive in a real combat situation. At the end of each section are a number of choices. The consequences of your decision are described in the next section. When you make the right decisions, morale improves and you are closer to completing your mission. When you make a bad decision, men die . . . men who are not going to be available for future battles.

FIGHTING BATTLES

This book includes a simple game system, which simulates combat and other military challenges. Playing the game adds an extra dimension of enjoyment by making you a participant in the adventure. You will need two six-sided dice, a pencil, and a sheet of paper to "play" along with this adventure.

COMBAT VALUES

In this book the force you command will consist of Emerald's Space Fleet, its crewmen, and marines. Each ship or man is assigned five values. These values provide the means of comparing the capabilities of the many different military units encountered in this book. These five values are:

Manpower

This value is the number of separate fighting parts of your force. Each unit of Manpower represents one man, ship, or part of a larger ship. Casualties are subtracted from Manpower.

Ordnance

The quality and power of the weapons used is reflected by their Ordnance Value. All members of a unit commanded will have the same Ordnance Value. In some cases you may command two or more units, each with a different Ordnance Value. In this book the Jupiter fleet consists of several classes of comparable smaller ships, nine drones, and two major ships that have exactly twice the Ordnance Value of the smaller craft.

Attack Strength

This value indicates the ability of the unit to attack an opponent. It is determined by multiplying Manpower by Ordnance (Manpower × Ordnance = Attack Strength). This value can be different for every battle. It will decrease as Manpower is lost and increase if reinforcements are received.

Melee Strength

This is the hand-to-hand combat value of each member of the unit. In the case of a squad of mercenaries, it represents the martial-arts skill and training of each man. In crewed units such as tanks or spaceships, it represents the fighting ability of the members of the crew and could be used in an assault on a spaceport or to defend against boarders. Melee Strength replaces Ordnance Value when determining the Attack Strength of a unit in hand-to-hand combat.

Stealth

This value measures how well the members of your unit can avoid detection. It represents the individual skill of each soldier or the Electronic Counter Measures (ECM) of each spaceship. The Stealth Value for your unit will be the same for each member of the unit. You would employ stealth to avoid detection by the enemy.

Morale

This value reflects the fighting spirit of your troops. Success in battle may raise this value. Unpopular decisions or severe losses can lower it. If you order your unit to attempt something unusually dangerous, the outcome may be affected by their morale level. For example, in a situation where *you* are Teddy Roosevelt and have just ordered the Rough Riders to charge up San Juan Hill, the directions would read:

Roll two six-sided dice.
If the total rolled is the same as, or less than, the Rough Riders' Morale Value, turn to section 24.

If the value rolled is greater than their current Morale Value, turn to section 31.

In section 24, the riders follow you as Teddy Roosevelt up the hill and into history.

In section 31, they have lost faith in you and refuse to attack.

THE COMBAT PROCEDURE

When your unit finds itself in a combat situation, use the following procedure to determine victory or defeat. This system uses a random dice roll combined with the situation itself to determine the casualties on both sides. You roll first for yourself and then for the enemy. The unit you command always fires first unless otherwise stated.

The steps to fight a combat are:

1. Compute the Attack Strength of your unit and the opposition (Manpower × Ordnance or Melee Value). The manpower changes as you suffer losses. The Ordnance Value remains constant.

2. Casualties will be determined according to charts found at the end of this book. The description of the battle will tell you which chart to use. You must turn to the proper chart before you can fight the battle.

3. Roll two six-sided dice and total the result.

4. Find the Attack Strength of the unit at the top of the chart and the total of the dice rolled on the left-hand column of the chart. The number found where the column and row intersect is the number of casualties inflicted.

5. Repeat for your opponent's side, alternating attacks until all of one side is eliminated.

When you are told there is a combat situation, you will be given all the information needed for both your command and their opponent. Also listed are any unusual factors and what effect they will have on the battle. All combat is resolved by a dice roll and the charts included at the end of this book.

Here is an example of a complete combat:

Hammer's Slammers have come under fire from a force defending a ridge that crosses their line of advance. Alois Hammer has ordered your company of tanks to attack.

Slammers fire using Chart B.

Locals fire using Chart D with a Combat Strength of 3 and Manpower of 12 (this will give them an Attack Strength of 36).

To begin, you attack first and roll two *4s* for a total of 8. You have computed the current Attack Strength of your Slammers to be 64.

CHART B

Attack Strength

1–10 –20 –30 –40 –50 –60 –70 –80 –90 –100 101+

Dice
Roll

Dice Roll	1–10	–20	–30	–40	–50	–60	–70	–80	–90	–100	101+
2	0	0	0	1	1	1	2	2	2	3	4
3	0	0	1	1	1	2	2	2	3	3	4
4	0	1	1	1	2	2	2	3	3	3	4
5	1	1	1	2	2	2	3	3	3	4	5
6	1	1	2	2	2	3	3	3	4	4	5
7	1	2	2	2	3	3	3	4	4	4	5
8	2	2	2	3	3	3	4	4	4	5	6
9	2	2	3	3	3	4	4	4	5	5	6
10	2	3	3	3	4	4	4	5	5	5	6
11	3	3	3	4	4	4	5	5	5	6	7
12	3	3	4	4	4	5	5	6	6	7	8

Read down to 60–70 Attack Strength column until you get to the line for a dice roll of 8. The result is 4 casualties inflicted on your opponents by your company.

Subtract these casualties from the opposing force before determining their Attack Strength. (Combat is not simultaneous.) After subtracting the 4 casualties your company just inflicted on them, the enemy has a remaining Manpower Value of 8 (12 – 4 = 8). This gives them a remaining Attack Value of 24 (8 × 3 = 24). Roll two six-sided dice for the opposing force's attack and determine the casualties they cause your Slammers company. Subtract these casualties from your Manpower total on the Record Sheet. This ends one "round" of combat. Repeat the process for each round. Each time a unit receives a casualty, it will have a lower value for Attack Strength. There will be that many fewer men, tanks, spaceships, or whatever firing.

Continue alternating fire rolls, recalculating the Attack Strength each time to account for casualties, until one side or the other has lost all of its manpower or special conditions (given in the text) apply. When this occurs, the battle is over. Losses are permanent and losses from your unit should be subtracted from their total Manpower on the record sheet.

SNEAKING, HIDING, AND OTHER RECKLESS ACTS

To determine if a unit is successful in any attempt relating to stealth or morale, roll two six-sided dice. If the total rolled is greater than the value listed for the unit, the attempt fails. If the total of the two dice is the same as or less than the current value, the attempt succeeds or the action goes undetected. For example:

Rico decides his squad of Mobile Infantry (MI) will try to penetrate the bughole unseen. MI have a stealth value of 8. A roll of 8 or less on two six-sided dice is needed to succeed. The dice are rolled and the result is a 4 and a 2 for a total of 6. They are able to avoid detection by the bug guards.

If all of this is clear, then you are ready to turn to section 1 and take command. If you'd like another example of play, read on:

You are in command of a ten-man U.S. Army patrol in France, World War II, fall 1944 . . . fade to the distant sound of artillery fire.

1st Squad
2nd Platoon
B Company
29th Division
U.S. Army

Manpower 10
Ordnance 4

Stealth 9

Morale 10 (after all, we're winning)

Melee 5

This squad has an initial Attack Strength of 40 (4 × 10) in a firefight. It has an initial Attack Strength of 50 in a hand-to-hand melee (5 × 10).

Your squad is ordered to penetrate enemy lines to determine if a battery of artillery is concealed in the village of Soissons. There are no known German positions and the front is still fluid. You have crossed into Nazi-controlled territory.

You had walked a long way since Omaha beach and your feet were sore. As the squad moved through the last of the pickets you signaled for Corey Roberts to take the point. The trooper freed his M1 and trotted on ahead. The sun had just risen; the air was filled with the acrid odor of cordite from our own artillery. Somewhere, a few miles in the rear, you could hear the roar of a battery firing on some unseen target. Everyone hoped it would distract the Nazis, but knew better.

The next few hundred yards were uneventful. The front was new here; neither side had had time to establish a continuous line. Suddenly Lewis whispered an urgent command and everyone froze. Up ahead Roberts was crouched behind a tree, gesturing at a clump of bushes a few yards ahead of him.

After a few tense moments you could see the first German as he emerged from the bushes. Moments later three more followed. All were armed with submachine guns and wore the black uniforms of the SS. They were moving very cautiously. The Germans didn't appear to have spotted you.

If you attack the German patrol, turn to section 41.

If you wish to remain concealed and let them pass, turn to section 42.

41

The Americans attack on Chart B.

The Germans fire back on Chart D. Their submachine guns have a firepower of 6, giving them an initial Attack Strength of 24.

If you win the battle, turn to section 55

If you are defeated, turn to section 29.

The American patrol attacks first. You roll two six-sided dice and total them. They are a 4 and a 3 for a total of 7. Looking down the column for an Attack Strength of 40 until you reach the row for a dice roll of 7, we see you killed 2 of the Nazis.

You would then roll for the 2 remaining Germans' return fire. In this case you roll a 4 and a 5 for a total of 9. Since each German with an SMG has an Ordnance Value of 6, this gives the 2 men a remaining Attack Strength of 12 (2×6). Looking in the 1–20 column of Chart D next to the 9, we see they cause 1 casualty. One man is subtracted from the Manpower of the American patrol, leaving a total now of 9 men and an Attack Strength of 36 ($9 \times 4 = 36$, as the Ordnance Value of the remaining men never changes).

This completes one round of combat.

A second round is then begun with the Americans again firing first. Two six-sided dice are rolled for a total of 10. Checking on Chart B in the 30–40 column for a roll of 10, we find that this fire was sufficient to kill three more Nazis. As only 2 remained, the combat is over immediately (there being no return fire from the SS troopers since they are all dead). You would then turn to section 55.

42

Roll two six-sided dice. If the total is the same as or less than 9, turn to section 46.

If the total is greater than 9, turn to section 47.

Here you are trying to remain undetected and so will be rolling against the squad's value for Stealth, which is a 9. Any total except a 10, 11, or 12 would indicate success. If the two dice were to roll a 5 and a 2 for a total of 7, your patrol will escape detection. You would then turn to section 46 and continue the mission.

Special Rules for *Cut by Emerald*

USJ SHIPS' ORDNANCE VALUES

All ships except the cruisers and drones have an Ordnance Value of 7. The cruisers have an Ordnance Value of 14 and should be counted as 2 ships ($2 \times 7 = 14$) when computing the Ordnance Value of the fleet firing as a whole. A drone is expended when fired, and for that round only has an ordnance value of 21. Once a drone is used, it is destroyed and should be crossed off your record sheet. Treat a drone, on the turn expended, as 3 ships firing ($3 \times 7 = 21$).

USJ LOSSES

The type of ship that must be taken as a loss when a hit is made on the USJ fleet will often be specified in the text. If no type is specified, then the loss may be taken by any ship that was engaged in the combat. This can only include drones that have not yet attacked, as these self-destruct during their attack. You may attack with the drones only when instructed to do so. Even though cruisers fire as 2 ships, they count as only 1 ship for losses. The *Inverness* must be the last ship taken as a loss. When it is destroyed, the game is over and you should turn to section 29. The minesweeper, *Risk,* must be taken as the second to last, as it tends to avoid most combat.

A record sheet has been provided to assist you in keeping track of the USJ ships remaining.

TIME

Emerald not only has to cross the hostile territory, but also be in place for the flank attack just as Hope and the main fleet pass by. Each action or series of actions in the adventure takes time. At the end of certain sections, you will be given the amount of time that has passed. A record sheet, marked off in half-hour segments, has been included to assist you in keeping track of the time you expend. If more than 12 hours pass before you reach the planned battlefield, you have failed and should turn to section 29.

FINAL FORCE STRENGTH

When arriving at the battlefield, your fleet must consist of no less than 5 ships of any class. As the *Inverness* and *Risk* are the last 2 ships that can be taken as losses, they will be among these ships. If, when asked, your fleet has fallen below this level of strength, then there is not enough force left to make an effective flanking attack and you have failed. In this case you should turn to section 29 and follow the instructions given there.

You are now ready to assume command. Turn to section 1.

TABLE I

SHIP LOSS RECORD SHEET

Ship	Ordnance Value	Type
Inverness	14*	Cruiser
Brooksville	14*	"
Discovered Check	7	Destroyer
Nightwing	7	"
Bear	7	"
Golden State	7	"
Silver Dawn	7	"
Wolf	7	"
Windemere	7	Escort
Charleston	7	"
Kukri	7	"
Scimitar	7	"
Pike	7	"
Lance	7	"
Monticello	7	"
Huntington	7	"
Risk	7	Minesweeper
Sparrowhawk	7	Assault Ships
Hummingbird	7	"
Bluejay	7	"
Raven	7	"
Tug 1	0	Unarmed Tug**
Tug 2	0	"
Tug 3	0	"
Drones (9)	21 each***	Unmanned Drone

Drone 1	Drone 2	Drone 3
Drone 4	Drone 5	Drone 6
Drone 7	Drone 8	Drone 9

Cross off each ship as it is lost.

*Count as 2 ships for computing Attack Value, one ship for losses.
**A tug may pull no more than 3 drones. If there are not enough tugs to carry drones, they are lost.
***Counts as 3 ships when computing Attack Value for one round only. Do not count for losses from enemy fire.

TABLE II

COMBAT VALUES
BY
SHIP'S CLASS

	Emerald's Fleet
Fleet Stealth Value	8
Fleet Morale	9

	Cruisers
Ordnance Value	14
Stealth Value	8
Melee Value	7

Large ships with a heavy weight of guns.

	Destroyers
Ordnance Value	7
Stealth Value	7
Melee Value	6

Versatile ships with lighter guns, mainly employ torps/missiles in combat. The true workhorses of the USJ navy.

	Escorts/Corvettes
Ordnance Value	7
Stealth Value	9
Melee Value	6

Primarily gun platforms with some limits on ammunition and supplies. Often act independently on convoy duty. Often need to be resupplied after a major engagement. Crowded and uncomfortable on long voyages.

	Birds/Long-Range Assault Fighters (sometimes called "chicks")
Ordnance Value	7
Stealth Value	9
Melee Value	—

Crewed by two men, these fighters are severely restricted to the amount of ammunition and fuel they carry. Being not much more than guns and engine they are extremely unpleasant on voyages lasting more than a few days. They depend almost entirely on speed and maneuverability for defense, something less than a perfect shield in an age of computer-targeted smart missiles. These are the smallest USJ military craft capable of sustained interplanetary flight.

	Minesweeper
Ordnance Value	7
Stealth Value	8
Melee Value	5

A workhorse three times the size of a destroyer, but with about the same armament. This class boasts specially mounted Gatlings, which fire shrapnel mixed with magnetic discs and short-burst, wide-spectrum radio "announcers" into suspected mine fields, detonating virtually all types of space mines.

	Tugs
Ordnance Value	0
Stealth Value	8
Melee Value	0

Civilian ships converted for naval use, they carry up to three drones, but are themselves unarmed.

	Drones
Ordnance Value	21
Stealth Value	N/A
Melee Value	N/A

This type of combat craft is relatively new to the USJ navy. Drones are massive missiles; on their noses are mounted a number of small cannon. They also contain 40 to 48 short-range homing missiles, designed to overwhelm the enemy's defenses. A drone is capable of extremely rapid motion, but due to limited fuel (everything is packed with guns and missiles) can sustain combat speed for less than three minutes.

These unmanned craft are designed to be carried to battle in a *Hiroshima*-class battleship, or larger, from which they are controlled. Occasionally a tug can be used for transport. When this is done, they are controlled from the formation's flagship.

TABLE III

ELAPSED TIME CHART

Mark off the time as it passes. You will be told when to do so in the text.

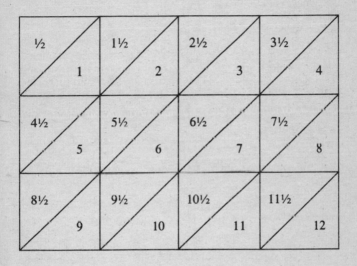

CHART A

Dice Roll	1–10	–20	–30	–40	–50	–60	–70	–80	–90	–100	101+
2	0	0	0	1	2	2	2	3	4	5	6
3	0	1	2	2	2	3	4	5	6	7	7
4	1	2	2	2	3	3	4	5	6	7	8
5	2	2	2	3	3	4	5	5	6	7	8
6	2	2	2	3	4	4	5	6	7	7	8
7	2	2	3	4	4	5	5	6	7	8	8
8	2	3	3	4	4	5	6	6	7	8	9
9	3	3	4	4	5	5	6	7	8	8	9
10	3	4	4	5	5	6	7	7	8	9	10
11	3	4	4	5	6	6	7	8	9	10	11
12	4	4	5	6	7	7	8	9	10	11	12

CHART B

Dice Roll	1–10	–20	–30	–40	–50	–60	–70	–80	–90	–100	101+
2	0	0	0	1	1	1	2	2	2	3	4
3	0	0	1	1	1	2	2	2	3	3	4
4	0	1	1	1	2	2	2	3	3	3	4
5	1	1	1	2	2	2	3	3	3	4	5
6	1	1	2	2	2	3	3	3	4	4	5
7	1	2	2	2	3	3	3	4	4	4	5
8	2	2	2	3	3	3	4	4	4	5	6
9	2	2	3	3	3	4	4	4	5	5	6
10	2	3	3	3	4	4	4	5	5	5	6
11	3	3	3	4	4	4	5	5	5	6	7
12	3	3	4	4	4	5	5	6	6	7	8

CHART C

Dice Roll	1–10	–20	–30	–40	–50	–60	–70	–80	–90	–100	101+
2	0	0	0	0	0	1	1	1	2	2	2
3	0	0	0	0	1	1	1	2	2	2	3
4	0	0	0	1	1	1	2	2	2	3	3
5	0	0	1	1	1	2	2	2	3	3	4
6	0	1	1	1	2	2	2	3	3	3	4
7	1	1	1	2	2	2	3	3	3	4	5
8	1	1	2	2	2	3	3	3	4	4	5
9	1	2	2	2	3	3	3	4	4	5	5
10	2	2	2	3	3	3	4	4	4	5	6
11	2	2	3	3	3	4	4	4	5	5	6
12	2	3	3	3	4	4	4	5	5	6	7

CHART D

Dice Roll	1–10	–20	–30	–40	–50	–60	–70	–80	–90	–100	101+
2	0	0	0	0	0	0	0	1	1	1	2
3	0	0	0	0	0	0	1	1	1	2	2
4	0	0	0	0	0	1	1	1	2	2	2
5	0	0	0	0	1	1	1	2	2	2	3
6	0	0	0	1	1	1	2	2	2	3	3
7	0	0	1	1	1	2	2	2	3	3	4
8	0	1	1	1	2	2	2	3	3	4	4
9	1	1	1	2	2	2	3	3	3	4	5
10	1	1	2	2	2	3	3	3	4	4	5
11	1	2	2	2	3	3	3	4	4	5	5
12	2	2	2	3	3	3	4	4	5	5	6

CHART E

Dice Roll	1–10	–20	–30	–40	–50	–60	–70	–80	–90	–100	101+
2	0	0	0	0	0	0	0	0	0	1	1
3	0	0	0	0	0	0	0	0	1	1	1
4	0	0	0	0	0	0	0	1	1	1	2
5	0	0	0	0	0	0	1	1	1	2	2
6	0	0	0	0	0	1	1	1	1	2	2
7	0	0	0	0	1	1	1	1	2	2	2
8	0	0	0	1	1	1	1	2	2	2	2
9	0	0	1	1	1	1	2	2	2	2	2
10	0	1	1	1	1	2	2	2	2	2	3
11	1	1	1	1	2	2	2	2	2	2	3
12	1	1	1	2	2	2	2	2	2	3	3

CHART F

Dice Roll	1–10	–20	–30	–40	–50	–60	–70	–80	–90	–100	101+
2	0	0	0	0	0	0	0	0	0	0	0
3	0	0	0	0	0	0	0	0	0	0	0
4	0	0	0	0	0	0	0	0	0	0	0
5	0	0	0	0	0	0	0	0	0	0	0
6	0	0	0	0	0	0	0	0	0	0	1
7	0	0	0	0	0	0	0	0	0	0	1
8	0	0	0	0	0	0	0	0	0	1	1
9	0	0	0	0	0	0	0	0	1	1	1
10	0	0	0	0	0	0	0	1	1	1	1
11	1	1	1	1	1	1	1	1	1	1	2
12	1	1	1	1	1	1	1	1	1	2	3

CHART G

Dice Roll	1–10	–20	–30	–40	–50	–60	–70	–80	–90	–100	101+
2	0	0	0	0	0	0	0	0	0	0	0
3	0	0	0	0	0	0	0	0	0	0	0
4	0	0	0	0	0	0	0	0	0	0	0
5	0	0	0	0	0	0	0	0	0	0	0
6	0	0	0	0	0	0	0	0	0	0	0
7	0	0	0	0	0	0	0	0	0	0	0
8	0	0	0	0	0	0	0	0	0	0	0
9	0	0	0	0	0	0	0	0	0	0	0
10	0	0	0	0	0	0	0	0	0	0	1
11	0	0	0	0	0	0	0	0	0	1	1
12	1	1	1	1	1	1	1	1	1	1	1

— 1 —

Piracy had plagued the Belt for decades. So long as the criminals preyed off each other, and the helpless, the major powers tended to leave them alone. But every now and then some of the less bright of these brigands overstepped their bounds.

The daughter of an influential United States of Jupiter family was held hostage and brutalized. The navy was called in to clean out the Juclip and Belt sectors. They assigned a "wild card" captain named Hope Hubris to the mission. It was a no-lose situation for the navy. If he screwed up, he was out and no loss as far as the navy was concerned. If he succeeded, he could have his headline, and the pirate problem would be solved.

Hubris's own antipirate crusade has been under way for several years. Because of Hope Hubris's well-planned strategies and the efforts of the rat pack of "losers" he has gathered and those willing to gamble big on an unparalleled career move, they have kicked ass so far, largely cleaning up the pirate problem. One major enemy remains, one with a distinguished fleet nearly as large as, or larger than the USJ (United States of Jupiter) fleet, one with allies, and with reasonably good commanders: the Marianas.

The senior command staff of the task force is assembled in the wardroom aboard the *Sawfish*—all except their commanding officer, Captain Hope Hubris.

"I presume we have the commodore safely tucked in bed," comments the officer in charge, opening the meeting. The speaker is Lieutenant Commander Emerald Sheller, a tough career officer in her late twenties, a black woman who has gained rank and respect despite—or perhaps because of—the color and sex discrimination that still exist in the modern space fleet. The commodore in question is her commanding officer, Captain Hope Hubris, who is entitled to that archaic title because he is not captain of the *Sawfish*, but has the rank of captain and is in command of the task force.

The officer to Emerald's left suppresses a rather wry grin. This woman's skin seems fair next to Emerald's fine, coffee-dark features, but she, too, has fought for her bars. Spirit Hubris is the commodore's sister, and has worked her way up past the special problems of a Hispanic emigrant, made more difficult given the current political picture of the solar system.

"I'm sure he's doing just fine with his pirate bride," Spirit leers.

Her fellow officers respectfully ignore her bitterness. Captain Hubris has just married the beautiful, but not entirely willing, daughter of a pirate chieftain in order to forge vital political ties. The navy could ignore and even deny the specifics of the alliance, and probably get a free shot at the captain for going native, but the powers-that-be in the government would use the peace agreement for their own gains. At the moment, Captain Hubris could care less. He is . . . busy elsewhere.

"Keeping Hope out of this was a stroke of genius," Emerald comments. Her husband and fellow officer, Lieutenant Commander Mondy, nods in acknowledgment.

It has been decided to use the ancient Mongol strategy for the upcoming battle. The enemy, a pirate nation based on a group of planetoids collectively called the Marianas after the Terran island chain, will, it is hoped, fall into the errors that his model, Bela of Hungary, had committed over a millennium ago. Captain Hubris would act as the devil's advocate, playing Bela and trying to beat his own staff at their game. Hopefully the staff will later be able to out-psych the real enemy, based on the captain's insights.

Nervousness makes Mondy, the intelligence staff officer, sound more forceful than usual. "It is essential to the part the captain plays that he does not get wind of this flanking action."

"Don't worry. His little pirate maiden will keep him busy. She has a very clear picture of what her future could hold as a commissioned officer and Jupe citizen. Believe me, the native life isn't all it's cracked up to be. She isn't going to blow her chance to be an officer and a lady. She'll keep him holed up in there until morning," Emerald insists, with a knowing smirk.

The officers grin and someone comments about inadvertent double entendre.

"Okay, okay, down to business." Emerald's voice cracks like a whip. Beyond the usual military crispness, which Sheller

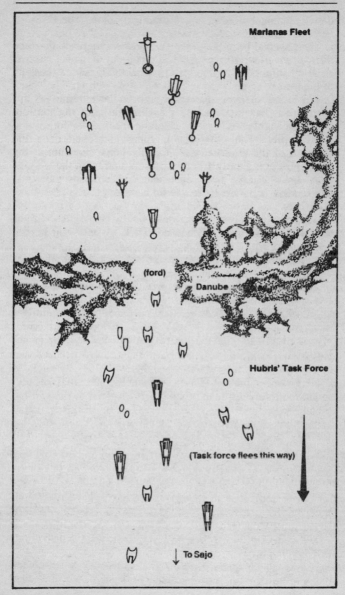

has in abundance, there is a shattering tension. The fleet has been on the run for five days.

The plan had been this: Like the Mongols in 1241, the Jupe fleet approached the entrenched position of the Marianas fleet, "fording a river," although in actuality it was passing through a clear place in a band of space debris. They then halted to the far side of another and far larger band of this orbiting sandstorm, which they had given the code name of "Danube."

As expected, the Marianas command had held their entrenched position, allowing the USJ fleet to weaken from lack of supplies, or simply to outwait them until they left. Three days ago the USJ task force retreated a short way in a strategic move. Whether it was from impatience, audacity, or the rumor that a considerable fleet of allies was on its way to support them, the Marianas sent out a small strike force across the "Danube." It had consisted of only one cruiser and four escorts.

Hubris ordered his task force not to attack this smaller and weaker force, but to continue to flee. This drew out the rest of the Marianas fleet. For the past five days the USJ Navy had appeared to be in full and disordered retreat, staying just ahead of the larger pirate fleet. Finally they reached the first of these debris "rivers," which was code named "Sajo" after a historical river that figured in the original Hungarian battle.

Emerald had commanded the fleet to retreat through the clear passage through which they had made their assault. Then she ordered the fleet to decelerate and hold the opening, thus creating something of an impasse, with the larger Marianas force being unable to use their greater numbers in the narrow gap. Currently, both forces sat, the USJ fleet on one side of the Sajo and the Marianas fleet on the other.

Now Emerald was about to enter into the big gamble that would win or lose this battle.

"Okay," she continues. "Listen up." She produces a lap computer with a small display. "I don't want anything online. No leaks. Captain," she addresses the commander who is captain of the *Sawfish*, "I'll give you my coordinates in case this doesn't work. Use them if you survive, which won't be likely, and if you have any desire to bail me out. But I'm only giving you sealed hard copy. Don't enter them into the computer except on your personal password."

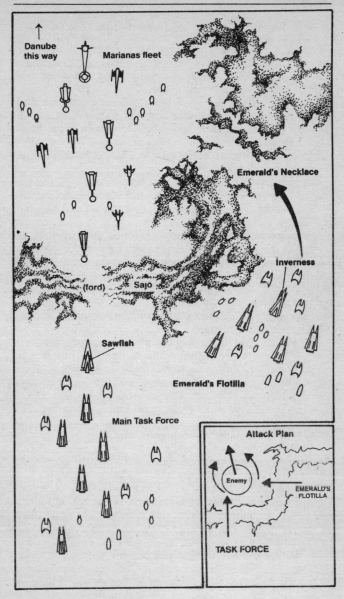

Danube this way

Marianas fleet

Emerald's Necklace

Inverness

(ford) Sajo

Sawfish

Emerald's Flotilla

Main Task Force

Attack Plan

Enemy

EMERALD'S FLOTILLA

TASK FORCE

"Agreed."

"This is the drill." She pulls out the stylus and touches the computer screen in several places. Then she taps in a code on the keyboard, and a map of the region comes up. She changes the view and scale a couple of times and then, satisfied, she sets the display down for all to see.

"I've had scouts out since we approached Sajo the first time. This is what we've found. About six hours at 2.8 G, let's call it upstream, there is"—she fiddles with the stylus—"here, see . . ."

Mondy sees it right off, but there is a lack of intelligence in some of his colleagues' eyes.

Emerald rotates the view. Then it becomes clear. The route she has outlined ends on the flank of the Marianas' formation. With the dust and ice, they will be unseen until the last possible moment.

"It's hard to find. That's why it isn't on the maps. As far as we can tell it's a good clear passage, but tricky. There are a couple of nasty chunks of space rock. Ice mostly, I'd guess, and between the erratic orbits, and the cue-ball effect . . . well, you can see. But it seems to have stayed clear, and I've been establishing a data base and getting some satisfactory analyses. My guess is that it is a semipermanent feature, but one that was never mapped.

"If we can pass through there unseen, we'd be on their flank. *If* the route stays open, and *if* we survive combat with any stray pirates, and *if* they aren't warned, and *if* they don't attack while I'm out of support range, and *if* we have enough force left to make a difference when we get there. But then if those remaining here attack at the same time . . ." she finishes hopefully.

"Do we get to name it?" someone wisecracks.

"Let's call it the Emerald's Cut," Phist, the logistics officer and part-time mechanic, suggests. "Where the pirates will be cut by something harder than a diamond, our Emerald."

Emerald has never worn any jewelry and Phist knows it. The stark lines of her uniform would never allow it and when she is out of uniform—well, on those occasions jewelry would just get in the way. Smiling, she acknowledges the teasing comment as support from the rest of their closely knit team, support she will need to pull this off. Encouraged, she continues.

"This is the plan. We divide our firepower, the fast ships

go with me. The heavies, *Sawfish* and the *Hempstone Crater*, stay here. That gives you firepower and most of the drones. I'll take the destroyers, except the *Purple Mountain*, which is still being upgraded and will hold us back. The *Inverness* is my command ship. And I'll take those three souped-up tugs." She turned, and gave a rare smile to Phist. "You're a genius. How did you get the materials to revamp those wrecks to get three gee out of them? Never mind. Any questions?" She can feel her own confidence and enthusiasm growing.

"Yeah, Phist. We're supposed to shoot pirates," the *Sawfish* captain adds, grinning.

"Anyhow, I'll take most of the destroyer escorts and torpedo boats. I won't need much supply. The Marianas are likely to never miss the smaller ships so long as the heavies stay in sight and make plenty of noise. This will be a hit and run . . . well, actually, a run and hit. I'll take nothing that will slow us down; every minute we are away there is a greater chance the pirates will hit us while divided. I can use that one escort which was converted from a merchantman as an ammo ship. It'll hurt the crew's dignity, but the storage racks are still in place.

"I'll board at 2300 Terra Standard and disembark at 2400. What time do you expect to funnel back across the Sajo, Captain?" Emerald asks.

"We will start to reconfigure at 0700, but we're planning to go slow. With any luck, if the enemy picks up the motion it will look like we're leaving. We figure to get under way at 1000, but we need time to ferry the cruiser through as well. Let's say we should be in place and battle ready at 1200 straight up."

"Well, that's neat and tidy, but it's going to be a horse race. I'll attempt to bring my wing around the flank through Emerald's Cut and be in position to hit the enemy flank at 1200 hours tomorrow. Any questions? Ladies and gentlemen, let's hit the deck. Let's see if we can confuse Commodore Hubris, then go for the real thing. Dismissed."

It is now almost 2400 hours: You will now make the decisions for Lieutenant Commander Emerald Sheller in command of the flanking maneuver. You start with a total of 24 ships, which includes the Inverness. *(See Table I) All you have to do is be in position no later than twelve hours from launch, with at least the* Inverness *and five escort vessels of any class for a total of six ships. Along the way, you'll be given instructions to mark off time elapsed on your time chart. You have 12 hours to reach the battlefield in time. Any later and Hope's force will be crushed by the pirates.*

Go to section 2.

— 2 —

Mondy knocks on the hatch of the quarters he shares with his wife. This is no time to barge in.

"Yeah."

"Emerald, it's me."

She opens the door. She is dressed in battle grays, her kit packed beside her.

"I don't suppose I'll need much, but a change of socks is nice." Her voice is tight, her body tense, but it is an upbeat tension. This is what she lives for, is willing to die for. This is her job, and she wouldn't give it up for anything—or anybody.

"Watch your ass. I want it back in one piece." He, too, shares in the battle joy, for the first time in years. He was a reluctant combat soldier, but he now feels dignity in ridding the spaceways of criminals, and he feels pride in his companion and fellow officer. He gives her a quick but loving hug.

"I'll be back. See you tomorrow," she says, smiling; but the smile is empty, and her mind is already a million miles away.

He salutes her as she strides down the passage, her bag in one hand, and the case with her lap computer in the other.

She makes her way to the hangar deck, after joining some of her personal staff in the big freight elevator. They don't even make small talk as they proceed to the shuttle bay. They quickly launch and shuttle to the *Inverness*. The captain is waiting on deck.

"Request permission to come aboard, sir," the lieutenant commander snaps out, saluting the USJ flag mounted to the bulkhead.

The captain salutes her aboard, and they head straight for

the bridge, the other officers left to the duty officer for the changeless amenities.

As she accompanies Lieutenant Commander Bradford Hodges, the captain of the cruiser, Emerald muses that this timeless boarding ritual probably originated as a way of identifying crew from pirates. How little things change on the high seas!

"Where would you care to make your headquarters, ma'am?" the captain asks her, offering her the formality of her rank as a compliment. They have been friends for years.

He continues, "You are welcome on the bridge, but there is also a second command center below and amidships if you prefer."

"Bridge is fine, if you don't object, Captain," she tells him, returning the respect.

"We should be ready to launch at 0030. We're running a little late. Engineering tells me the new equipment is on board, and almost installed."

"Are we waiting for them to finish?"

"Mainly."

"Can we effect installation once we are away?"

"Yes, ma'am. It's more a matter of precaution that we be battle ready before launch."

She addresses the E6 at the communications console. "Are we on ready with the rest of the wing?"

"Confirmed with all but Hen Two and Three."

"Tell me the minute they clear."

"Yes, ma'am," the technician answers, without ever taking his eyes off the console.

"You have until we clear the rest of the wing, Captain. Then it's go. We're on a clock."

"Yes, ma'am."

"It's a go, ma'am. Repeat, Hen Two and Three are go."

The claxon goes off as the order "brace for gee" echoes through the ship.

The communications officer signals his tech, and the signal for launch is sent to each member of the wing. Up until now, ship-to-ship communications have been verbal. Now that the code is tapped in, and launch is coordinated by computer, each member of the wing becomes part of a giant bird, rising with grace from its position in the fleet and moving out into space.

Emerald thrills in the gee force. The shuddering engines

give birth to raw power as the *Inverness*'s thirteen kilotons fight to deny the laws Newton noted but never created. Emerald is slammed into the padded launch couch. For some men and women the driving force is money or sex. For her it is the navy; for all its bullshit, she feels more than alive immersed in its massive power and discipline. She knows that this strategy must succeed. And she has to facilitate the tactics to make it work. For herself. For her unit. For her service.

Before long, the internal inertial frame is equalized enough for everyone to start about their business. The first order is a sharp complaint from Engineering that some of the new equipment was too far along toward installation to be stowed and there was some damage at launch.

Emerald takes a quick survey of her station, puts the next ranking line officer from her small staff in charge, and personally goes below.

The Engineering officer is a tall gangly man, a fact she surmises by the length of the legs emerging from under the twisted command console. He pulls himself out, hands his socket wrench to an enlisted man, and glowers at her.

"Ma'am—" he begins with measured control.

"Please, Lieutenant. Let me apologize," she interrupts, smiling in a reassuring way. There is no point making enemies, and she would have been just as livid if someone had screwed over one of her assigned operations. "I gave you the wet end of the stick. No lie. We are in a serious time bind. Do what you can here. I'll take full responsibility for the damage and its consequences. But we couldn't delay launch."

Somewhat mollified, or at least too boxed in to argue, the lieutenant asks, "If you allow me, ma'am, these look like drone controls. Last time I looked we weren't a carrier."

"That's right, Lieutenant," she answers, then turns without comment and heads back to her command, leaving the officer more puzzled than angry.

She has learned what she needed to know. Six drone command modules are in place, one is dubious but probably not in irreparable condition, and the other two are even now being dragged against the ambient gee forces, out of their webbing and onto the deck. So far, so good.

She returns to the bridge, where the maneuver is on course and on time.

The captain comes over to her console and says, "I had an

ensign take your bag to Lieutenant Dixon's quarters. She's the analyst you requested. We don't have VIP quarters set up, and I thought you wouldn't mind bunking with the lieutenant. I doubt any of us are going to get any rest, anyhow."

"Thank you, Brad. I'm sure that will be fine."

He waves a young woman from her post. She turns her console over to a tech, and obeys the order. "Lieutenant Dixon, why don't you show Commander Sheller to your quarters. This may be all the quiet we get."

"Yes, sir." As they make their way down from the bridge and through the ship to the officers' quarters, Emerald notes that the sturdy young woman wears a shiny new academy ring.

"What's a nice girl like you doing in a chicken-shit unit like this?" Emerald asks, smiling.

The officer guffaws. "When I graduated, damn near the top of my class, I was offered a staff position in Intelligence on the New Washington bubble, or a staff position on a navigational bubble. I wanted a line career and upward mobility. This rat pack offered advancement and battle experience. And pretty good drinking buddies."

Emerald agrees with the woman. This is the unit where careers can be made—or lost. But she promises herself that if she ever attains flag rank, she will do what she can for women like Dixon.

The cabin is small, but comfortable. Emerald quickly stows her gear, and they return to the bridge. Just as Emerald settles again into her command post, radar announces, "Bogey at two o'clock."

The captain, the exec, and Emerald are first around the large display. Indeed there is a blip, distinguished among the space junk by its speed and course.

"Well?" the captain asks.

"Don't know yet, sir. Could be a rock. But it doesn't move like a rock. No hot spots, but life readings are hard to get through a hull." When all is said and done, this is still as much an art as a science. With maybe a little magic for good measure.

"I want a regression course. Where is it coming from?"

The display appears on the screen in microseconds, but it doesn't help much.

"Ma'am," Dixon offers, still tapping data into a spreadsheet.

"There is a large planetoid somewhat upriver. If that thing is a vessel, it could have come from there."

"Colonists? Miners?" Emerald muses, but it is impossible to guess if it belongs to peaceful colonists, or if it is a stray salvage ship of the type that creates its own salvage.

Emerald quickly calls a war council. "If it is a raider, we could just let it come to us. That would be fuel and time efficient. But if it's a scout ship for the Marianas or one of its allies, then we're in deep shit if it gets a close look at us and gets a message out. Chances are it's a mining ship on a supply run and the whole thing is a waste of effort. What do you think?"

The electronic instrument officer is asked to brief the staff on what he can determine from the output, and Dixon adds what little is known about the area. They cannot break communication silence to get updates from the main body of the fleet.

"Sir, the bogey has changed course. That's no rock. It's paralleling our movement."

If Emerald decides to wait it out, go to Section 3.

If Emerald decides to order ships to chase the bogey down, go to section 4.

— 3 —

"Let's sit on it a bit. Let me know if there's any change."

Emerald is motionless, eyes riveted on the radar screen, wondering how such a noisy place as a space cruiser could feel so silent, despite the throbbing engines, the soft whirr of the environmental systems, and the rhythmic click of keyboards and switches.

The measured monotone of the EIO breaks the silence.

"It's moving again. It's coming for us."

If Emerald reconsiders and orders the bogey to be chased down, go to section 4.

If she decides to wait, go to section 5.

— 4 —

"Okay, that's it. At that range, if we deploy the destroyer *Golden State,* how long has she got to catch up?"

The numbers are already being entered on the simulator. Lieutenant Dixon is on the console. "At full power, she has one hour forty-nine minutes to rendezvous, engage, and start back. The bogey is thirty-two minutes to contact, given destroyer launch in seven minutes. Sir, if you put one up, perhaps you might commit two more. I suggest an escort of the *Windemere* and the *Charleston.* They have commensurate gee ratings and they will triple firepower."

"Excellent, lieutenant." Emerald turns to the communications officer, and says, "Give the order, Commander. Give me the horn." She is patched in to the squad leader. "Captain. You have to maintain long-range radio silence on this one. After you leave the fleet you're on your own. Unless it is a senior citizens' pleasure cruiser, blow that bogey up. Cripple it if you're unsure. But in any case, you have one hour and forty-one minutes to get in, get it, and get out. Copy?"

He rogers her message.

"Sir, that was one hour, forty-nine minutes," Dixon corrects her.

"I lied," Emerald explains with a wicked grin.

While the command staff on the bridge of the *Inverness* sweats, Lieutenant Commander John Aburto, captain of the *Golden State,* moves out with his two escorts.

"Full gee, let her rip," he commands. Short-range communications are set up between his command ship and the two escorts, but after the initial launch they, too, keep radio silence. Whoever this joker is, there is no point in announcing their arrival.

The *Golden State* approaches target range in record time, its two escorts being two minutes behind. The captain orders deceleration and sings out to his communications officer, "Open a hailing channel to the boat."

The vessel appears to be an old tanker, but it is clearly armed. That in itself is not surprising, since anything worth

stealing on this frontier is fair game, and there are no inno-
cents out here.

"This is Captain Aburto of the USJ *Golden State*. State
your name, registry, and business."

The two escorts have caught up and are fanning out in a
flanking pattern.

The vessel rotates slightly, its course now directly toward
the *Charleston*.

The captain bellows into the microphone, "Carlos, he's
going to hit you. *Move*." But as he warns the *Charleston*,
they can all see the blips of shells on the radar screen.

The enemy has fired first, with an Attack Strength of 8.

It fires using Chart C.

Use Chart C for the USJ ships' attack.

If the pirate destroys all three naval ships turn to section 6.

*If the pirate is destroyed, but the USJ Navy takes any losses,
turn to section 7.*

*If the pirate is destroyed without the loss of any USJ naval
vessels, turn to section 9.*

— 5 —

Emerald watches the vessel's approach. "Either it wants
help or it wants a good look. Nobody is dumb enough to hit a
fleet unless it is a kamikaze ship. Does anybody know if the
Marianas are hiring needle-head crazies?"

"No, ma'am," the Intelligence officer replies, "but there's
been some bad junk pushed in the last few months. It's a
percentage guess."

"Better safe than sorry. Captain, have a communications
channel opened."

The radioman sets up a hailing channel and says, "Sir, it's
open."

Emerald patches in on her console and announces in clipped

tones, "This is Lt. Commander Emerald Sheller aboard the USJ *Inverness*. Identify yourself or receive fire."

The response is a burst of laser cannon fire.

"That jackass is firing on us!" the captain bellows, stunned with disbelief.

"That's it. They're dead," Emerald snaps. "Course change for *Discovered Check,* the five escorts in *Check*'s sector. Pull back the tugs; move in the cruiser *Brooksville*. Blast the shit out of it."

The seven vessels go through the slow process of deceleration, course adjustment, and blastoff. They overtake the pirate and unload their firepower at the ship. The pirate has turned to escape and has therefore effectively disarmed itself, as its forward guns are the only powerful weapons it carries. The pirate is soon space debris, but precious time has been lost. It is already 0200.

Mark off 2 hours on your time chart.

Turn to Section 8.

— 6 —

On the bridge of the *Inverness* the officers and crew watch with horror as the blips representing *Golden State*, *Windemere*, and *Charleston* wink out. Whatever is out there is either tough or lucky. And good men have died.

"Shit!" Emerald mutters, then issues the command. "Chase it down. Course change for *Discovered Check* and the five escorts in the *Check*'s sector. Pull back the tugs, move in the cruiser *Brooksville*. Blast the shit out of it."

The seven vessels go through the slow process of deceleration, course adjustment, and blastoff. The pirate tries to radio someone ahead, but the ECM officer nods, smiling: jammed. The revenging ships overtake the pirate and unload their firepower and anger. The pirate has turned to escape and has therefore effectively disarmed itself, as its forward guns are the only powerful weapons it carries. Soon there remain only the USJ ships and an expanding sphere of space debris. But precious time has been lost, as well as men and vital fire-power. It is already 0230.

Mark off 2½ hours on your time chart.

Subtract 2 points from the entire fleet's Morale Value.

Turn to section 8.

— 7 —

The attack force returns to the fleet. Emerald receives the debriefing with the dispassion of a pro. The time for mourning will come if and when they complete this mission. Emerald had ordered the fleet to decelerate when she saw that this was not going to be a mop-up. Precious time has been lost, as well as vital firepower, and that hurts as much as the loss of her men. She looks at her chronometer. It is already 0200.

Mark off 2 hours on your time chart.

Subtract 1 point from the fleet's Morale Value.

Turn to section 8.

— 8 —

Emerald ponders the irony of it. Here in the vastness of space, why should they run into a stray pirate? Was it an accident, or was it a scout? She will probably never know, but now she is sure that this isn't going to be a pleasure cruise.

Turn to section 10.

— 9 —

The attack force returns in triumph. Aburto gives his report with the dispassion of a pro, but it is the first time he has commanded a squadron, and he is clearly a proud and happy officer. The wardrooms of the three ships will be filled with war stories at chow time, and morale is high. The fleet hasn't lost time or men on this, but Emerald is deeply disturbed. This is not going to be a pleasure cruise. She ponders the irony that, in the vastness of space, she would have run into a stray pirate so soon, and she wonders how many more little surprises lie ahead. It is now 0130, and they have a long way to go.

Add 1 point to Morale.

Note the passage of 1½ hours on your time chart.

Turn to section 10.

— 10 —

The nervous tension on the bridge doesn't subside, and even the normally calm manner of the men and women on the radar is less than a hundred percent steady. Every blip of space dust makes Emerald's heart jump.

"Coffee?" Hodges asks, handing Emerald a mug of the steaming brew. "Hope black is okay," he adds, with a clear twinkle in his eye.

"Black is just fine." she grins back, appreciating the open recognition of her color. She also appreciates the quality that makes him a fine officer. Yes, he respects her; and yes, she is under a lot of strain; and yes, this is his way of easing the strain.

She finishes the cup, gets up, and stretches. "Might as well hit the head, while I can."

"Good move. I think it was a Terran statesman named Churchill who said something about never missing an opportunity to piss. Don't know when the next one will come."

"Right." She leaves the bridge, jogging down the deck, trying to loosen up. She hears the sound of many boots jogging in unison, headed her way. Around the curve in the hall come the unit of Sea Slugs, the commando unit on board. They took the name when one of the men discovered a unit from old Earth called the Seals, who were reputed to be the toughest commandos ever trained. With that knowledge and a little zoological research, the Sea Slugs were born. If the Seals were sleek, the Slugs were disgusting, but that is only for them to say.

Their CO salutes as he jogs past, never missing a beat. Emerald routes her exercise back to the bridge, cheered by the lean, mean Slugs.

But trouble isn't over.

"Ma'am, the *Brooksville* is on the line."

"Put it through," Emerald orders, puzzled.

"This is Captain Lee here. We have a problem."

"Sheller here. What's up?"

"We have a red-line situation in the CT system. I am ordering a power down."

"Do it. Any guess what the cause is?"

"Not a clue. I'll get back to you as soon as we know anything. Over."

"Yeah, Jim, keep me posted. Out."

"Oh, great!" one of her lieutenants groans.

"Okay, let's think this out," Emerald instructs her staff. She is learning that command is as much teaching as performing, and that teaching in turn leads to more learning for herself as well. "Dixon, read it over to me."

"It's time versus firepower, the way I see it. The *Brooksville* is slower than the *Inverness* but carries more and bigger guns. It's a risk either way. If she is down for good, the longer we wait, the further behind schedule we get. If we leave her behind, she'll never catch up, unless she can get going, full speed, pretty quick. Then we'll be down one cruiser."

"Good, that's it. Now what do we do? Lieutenant?" she asks, responding to the bright look on the face of a lieutenant j.g. named Jackson.

"Could we hedge the bet? I mean, could we give them an

hour, or even half an hour, to assess the problem and then decide?''

The decision is Emerald's in the final analysis.

First mark 1 hour off your chart for cruising time.

If Emerald decides to leave the Brooksville *behind, go to section 11.*

If Emerald decides to decelerate the fleet while the Brooksville *looks for the problem, go to section 12.*

— 11 —

Emerald taps her stylus in a nervous staccato as she waits for the latest update from Engineering aboard the Big B. She doesn't want to leave the *Brooksville* behind, as the chance she will catch up is pretty slim, assuming the fleet doesn't run into another delay. On the other hand, if the techs start talking about a fourteen-hour repair, it is better to cut the loss now.

"*Brooksville* to *Inverness.*"

"Go ahead, *Brooksville.*"

"It looks like this is going to take a while. We think it's in the CT control. You know how touchy that is. It could be a ten-minute job, or we could have to strip it down to bolts."

"Thank you, *Brooksville.* Keep us posted."

Hodges looks at Emerald, raises an eyebrow, and sighs. The CT system, the central power source, is very touchy indeed, depending on matter/antimatter annihilation for energy. The *Brooksville* could go off like a bomb and take the fleet with it.

"Contact the *Brooksville,*" Emerald orders, her voice tired. "Wish them luck, and tell them to try to catch up. We may run into delays. If she's dead in the water until 0700, she might as well try to limp back to the main task force. Tell her."

The communications officer relays the message, and the fleet moves on.

You have not lost any time, but you have lost 1 of the 2 most powerful elements of your fleet. Cross it off on the Ship Loss Record Sheet.

Go to section 15.

— 12 —

Emerald taps her stylus in a nervous staccato as she waits for the latest update from Engineering aboard the *Big B*. She doesn't want to leave her behind, as the chance she will catch up is pretty slim, that is if the fleet doesn't have more delay. On the other hand, if the techs are talking about a fourteen-hour repair, it is better to cut the loss now.

"*Brooksville* to *Inverness*."

"Go ahead, *Brooksville*."

"It looks like this is going to take a while. We think it's in the CT control. You know how touchy that is. It could be a ten-minute job, or we could have to strip it down to bolts."

"Thank you, *Brooksville*. Keep us posted."

Hodges looks at Emerald, raises an eyebrow, and sighs. The CT system, the central power source, is very touchy indeed, depending on matter/antimatter annihilation for energy. The *Brooksville* could go off like a bomb and take the fleet with it.

"Contact the *Brooksville*," Emerald orders, taking the mike when they respond.

"Captain, I'm giving you thirty minutes."

"Understood, sir." He signs off, and the fleet commander orders her ships to decelerate.

Roll two six-sided dice.

If the total rolled is the same as or less than the fleet's value for Morale (in this case, "luck" is a better term), go to section 13.

If the total is greater than the fleet's value for Morale, go to section 14.

— 13 —

Within fifteen minutes the message comes through loud and clear.

"*Brooksville* to *Inverness*. Over."

The tone of the captain's voice tells the story before he gets the words out.

"We're back on-line. Thank God. A loose wire. One lousy loose wire. We're powering up and will be at full power in six minutes."

"That's a rog, *Brooksville*. Welcome back."

Mark ½ hour from your time chart and turn to section 16.

— 14 —

The minutes tick away like hours. "Contact the *Brooksville*," Emerald orders when the thirty minutes are up, her voice tired.

But even as she says it the console crackles, "*Brooksville* to *Inverness*. Over."

"*Inverness*. Over."

"We can't find it. We just can't find it." The frustration in the captain's voice hits the command crew like a blow.

"Wish them luck, and tell them to try to catch up," Emerald orders. "We may run into delays. If she's dead in the water until 0700, she might try to limp back to the main task force. Tell her."

The communications officer relays the message, and the fleet moves on.

You have lost ½ hour, and you have lost the second most powerful ship in your fleet. Cross the Brooksville *off on your Ship Loss Record Sheet.*

Turn to section 15.

— 15 —

The loss of the *Big B* hits the fleet hard. Despite the strict battle drill, the scuttlebutt goes through the fleet like wildfire.

Emerald hears some of it by the coffee urn in the wardroom, where she has gone for a few minutes of quiet. She heads directly for the bridge.

"Open a channel to all ships," she snaps.

She quickly confers with the captains, telling them she wishes to speak directly to their respective crews. With the courtesies out of the way, she gets on the public address system throughout the fleet.

"This is Commander Sheller speaking. I'm saying this once and once only. Every man jack of you, from E1 to O9, belay this scuttlebutt. The *Brooksville* is in no imminent danger, and the chances are she will rejoin the fleet before we hit our objective. In any case, you are all battle-tough space rats, not more than one cut above the pirates we're after. This is war, and you win some and lose some and that's the way it goes. Our morale is worth more than one ship, any ship, and our objective will be gained if the last living one of us has to do it alone in a vacuum suit with a pugil stick. This is 'hurry up and wait' time, but when we hit the enemy we will be one lean, mean fighting machine. Stay chill, men, stay chill."

She hears the scattered cheers and company battle cries resounding through the *Inverness* and knows that the other ships have been similarly affected.

When she returns to her station, Captain Hodges catches her eye and flicks her a salute. She smiles back at him as she returns the salute and resumes the long watch.

"Ma'am, the *Hummingbird* is reporting a faint communication signal from a position starboard to the fleet." Before she can respond, the communications officer's attention again turns to his console, and he adds, "That's confirmed by the *Sparrowhawk*."

"Patch me in. *Hummingbird*, this is Sheller. We copy. Wait, it's coming in directly."

The communications tech plays his console like a virtuoso, and the faint signal is enhanced.

"Help us, please. Anybody. Mayday. Mayday. This is the *Last Chance*. We're a mineral tanker. We've taken hull damage. Please, anybody. We're losing air."

"Oh, shit," Emerald spits, slamming her fist down on the table. "Check the registry."

"Done, ma'am," Dixon snaps out, efficiently, and the information appears on Emerald's screen.

"Oh, great. Mars registry. That's a catchall. Well, ladies and gentlemen, is it for real?"

Martian registry was indeed a problem. The lower safety standards and tax structure made it a godsend for penny-ante companies, but it also was a known cover registry for smugglers, spies, and bandits. Nonetheless, the problem remains that a mayday has been received, and it cannot be ignored.

"What have we got with any real firepower on that flank . . . and speed?"

"The *Discovered Check* is closest."

"Right. Deploy the *Check* with the two escorts who received the message, and pull off the two fastest, most heavily armed ships from that flank."

"The *Scimitar* and the . . . let's see. The *Kukri* has the firepower edge but the *Pike* has the speed." Dixon is earning her pay.

Emerald looks at the stats. "The *Pike*. Shuttle a dozen Slugs to the *Check*. I suspect we're going to be boarding the Mayday. What kind of time frame have we got?"

"The Mayday is some distance out. I figure"—Dixon taps at the simulator—"forty minutes from launch to contact. If we want to risk their playing catch-up, realistically they have about two hours all told. Unless we wait for them."

"Okay. Same drill as before. Give the order."

She listens as the command is relayed. It would take no more than ten minutes for the Slugs to mount up and blast off. The *Check* has more speed than anything else in the fleet, so they can delay their move for twenty minutes while the Slugs board.

Emerald watches the radar, again helpless, dependent on the training and intelligence of her officers to carry out the next tactical move. All she can do now is wait and watch the monitors. In the heat of a shipboard battle, any order from her, Emerald knows, will cause more confusion than it can do good.

* * *

On the bridge of the *Check*, Captain Undermeyer rubs his neck, trying to ignore the deep pain of the newly healed laser wound. This mission is all too familiar. Unless the Mayday opens fire, it will be a boarding mission, and the last time he boarded a ship he had nearly gotten himself killed. Well, that was last time and this was this time, and this time he was not going to cowboy. This time he will have Slugs on board.

"Are we secure for launch, spaceman?"

The enlisted man speaks into the intercom with the shuttle bay. The shuttle has already docked, and the Slugs are in the airlock, awaiting pressurization.

"The shuttle has undocked, and is under way, sir. Ready for launch."

Undermeyer gives the command and studies the radar screen as his squadron of five ships approaches the Mayday, fanning out into a crescent. The message is still being repeated. It sounds real enough, but . . .

They reach the Mayday after almost thirty-five minutes. At best it is going to be catch up on the way home.

"Open a channel, spaceman," the captain orders when he and his four escorts are in striking range and deployed.

"This is the USJ *Discovered Check*. Please identify yourself."

"This is the tanker *Last Chance*. Please help us. We're losing air."

Undermeyer looks at the hull on his screen. He can see the telltale "dust" of decompression. One of the plates is damaged near the cargo bay. He wonders why they haven't sealed off the bay. Something is wrong.

"Please clarify." He stalls for time and fishes for information.

"We were hit by a rock about a week ago. The bay was damaged, and the bay doors jammed. We jury-rigged a seal, but it isn't tight. We were low on supplies and fuel to begin with, which is why we were on a run into Juclip. We lost our cargo of ore, but worse, our environmental unit is damaged and our oxygen supply is leaking. We figured we had about four days, at best. Your finding us is a miracle."

"Prepare to be boarded," Undermeyer orders, maneuvering the *Check* to dock with the tanker and leaving the details for his exec to work out with its captain. So far it sounds good, but Undermeyer is a hard man to convince these days.

"Chief Perez." He stares at the massive Slug on the

screen. "Take your men and a unit of my men, armed with laser rifles and gas grenades. Secure the Mayday, if that is what it is."

The chief jogs his men into the airlock, the unit of spacemen jogging behind them. They cross, and board the *Last Chance*. So far, it is as advertised, but there is no welcoming committee.

"Jimenez," the chief hisses. He holds up two fingers, then points his rifle down the passage to the engine room.

Jimenez detaches his squad and gestures to one of his two Slugs, a muscular, stocky woman, to take the point. She runs down the deck to the first turn, and holds the corner as her buddy slams his body to the far corner. Jiminez brings up the rear, sliding around the corner, as his point moves out, followed by his patrol. Then they are out of sight.

The chief points to Popolus and hisses, "Greek, engine room," holding up two fingers. The Greek takes two Slugs and jogs down the gangway to the hatch leading below.

All are in pressure suits, and all have their pacifier-disrupters ready to fire.

The pacifier is an insidious little device, first developed to render criminals pliable for trial and rehabilitation. It soon became available to the criminal syndicates and was mass-marketed to thieves and pirates throughout the system. No amount of public pressure could create the legislation needed to freely supply the disrupter to honest, law-abiding civilians for self-protection, so except for those who can afford to support the brisk black market trade in them, colonists are easy pickings for raiders.

The communications button in Perez's ear crackles.

"Engine room secure, Chief," Greek reports.

Seconds later, Jimenez reports in. "Cargo bay looks like a bomb hit it, Chief. The bay doors are leaking like a sieve."

"Okay, join up and move up to general quarters deck. Spaceman," he barks, addressing the leader of the regular forces, "dispatch a patrol behind my men and hold both the engine room and cargo bay."

"Yes, Chief. You, you and you, with Hildeman. You three with Rosario. Move. The rest on me."

They move up to the bridge, leaving a reserve of three men in the airlock. There are five people on the bridge: two men, a woman, and two children. (They all look unkempt, except one of the men, who is dark and greasy and has beady eyes that won't meet anyone else's for long.)

"Who's in charge here?" the chief grunts, watching the greasy man and pointing his weapon in his general direction.

"I am." The dark man steps forward. "Thank God you're here. If you could help us repair, we'll be on our way. We certainly didn't wish to cause the navy any trouble."

"Right," the chief says, but in his mind he screams *Wrong*. These people are hostages, but their captors probably didn't expect to attract a fleet. The details of how the "leak" is controlled or how long they have been holding these people as bait is not clear, but what *is* clear is that there are a lot of very nasty pirates around somewhere.

"Chief, Hildeman. They've breached . . ."

"Shit!" the chief bellows, taking out the dark man with a blast from his laser rifle. "Hold these people. Secure the bridge." The regular forces take the bridge as the chief and six Slugs are bounding triple time toward the cargo bay.

"We are under attack," he radios the *Check*. Shouting orders to his two patrols as he runs, he and his men hit the doors of the cargo bay. The bay is filled with pirates.

Ship's Marines (Slugs)

Manpower 7
Ordnance 9
Melee 9
Stealth 5
Morale (same as fleet)

There are 7 Slugs in the bay, each heavily armed. Slugs have a Melee Value of 9 each. Their total Attack Strength is therefore 63 to start the attack.

Pirates

Manpower 21
Ordnance 2
Melee 2
Stealth 2
Morale 5

There are 21 pirates. They are variously armed, with average ordnance, and have a Melee Value of 2 apiece. They are not trained as a unit and are getting in each other's way, but they have the numbers and the position.

The Slugs fire from Chart B, the pirates using Chart E.

If the Slugs kill all the pirates, turn to section 17.

If the pirates win, turn to section 18.

— 16 —

"Ma'am, the *Hummingbird* is reporting a faint communication signal from a position starboard to the fleet." Before Emerald can respond, the communications officer's attention again turns to his console, and he adds, "That's confirmed by the *Sparrowhawk*."

"Patch me in. *Hummingbird*, this is Sheller. We copy. Wait, it's coming in direct."

The communications tech plays his console like a virtuoso, and the faint signal is enhanced.

"Help us, please. Anybody. Mayday. Mayday. This is the *Last Chance*. We're a mineral tanker. We've taken hull damage. Please, anybody. We are losing air."

"Oh, shit," Emerald spits, slamming her fist down on the table. "Check the registry."

"Done, ma'am," Dixon snaps out, efficiently, and the information appears on Emerald's screen.

"Oh, great. Mars registry. That's a catchall. Well, gentlemen, is it for real?"

Martian registry is indeed a problem. The lower safety standards and tax structure make it a godsend for penny-ante companies, but it is also a known cover registry for smugglers, spies, and bandits. Nonetheless, the problem remains that a Mayday has been received, and it cannot be ignored.

"What have we got with any real firepower on that flank . . . and speed?" Emerald asks.

"The *Discovered Check* is closest."

"Right. Deploy the *Check* with the two escorts who received the message, and pull off the two fastest, most heavily armed ships from that flank."

"The *Scimitar* and the . . . let's see. The *Kukri* has the firepower edge but the *Pike* has the speed." Dixon is earning her pay.

Emerald looks at the stats. "The *Pike*. Shuttle two dozen Slugs to the *Check*. I suspect we're going to be boarding that tanker. What kind of time frame have we got?"

"The Mayday is some distance out. I figure"—Dixon taps at the simulator—"forty minutes from launch to contact. If we want to risk their playing catch-up, realistically they have about two hours all told. Unless we wait for them."

"Okay. Same drill as before. Give the order."

She listens as the command is relayed. It would take no more than ten minutes for the Slugs to mount up and blast off. The *Check* has more speed than anything else in the fleet, so they can delay their move for twenty minutes while the Slugs board.

Emerald watches the radar, again helpless, dependent on the training and intelligence of her officers to carry out the next tactical move.

On the bridge of the *Check,* Captain Undermeyer rubs his neck, trying to ignore the deep pain of the newly healed laser wound. This routine is all too familiar. Unless the Mayday opens fire, it will be a boarding mission, and the last time he boarded a ship he had nearly gotten himself killed. Well, that was the last time and this was this time, and this time he was not going to cowboy. This time he will have Slugs on board.

"Are we secure for launch, spaceman?"

The enlisted man speaks into the intercom with the shuttle bay. The shuttle has already docked, and the Slugs are in the airlock, awaiting pressurization.

"The shuttle has undocked and is under way, sir. Ready for launch."

Undermeyer gives the command and studies the radar screen as his squadron of five ships approaches the Mayday, fanning out into a crescent. The message is still being repeated. It sounds real enough, but . . .

They reach the Mayday after almost thirty-five minutes. At best it is going to be catch up on the way home.

"Open a channel, spaceman," the captain orders when he and his four escorts are in striking range and deployed.

"This is the USJ *Discovered Check*. Please identify yourself."

"This is the tanker *Last Chance*. Please help us. We're losing air."

Undermeyer looks at the hull on his screen. He can see the

telltale "dust" of decompression. One of the plates is damaged near the cargo bay. He wonders why they haven't sealed off the bay. Something is wrong.

"Please clarify." He stalls for time and fishes for information.

"We were hit by a rock about a week ago. The bay was damaged, and the bay doors jammed. We jury-rigged a seal, but it isn't tight. We were low on supplies and fuel to begin with, which is why we were on a run into Juclip. We lost our cargo of ore, but worse, our environmental unit is damaged and our oxygen supply is leaking. We figure we had about four days, at best. Your finding us is a miracle."

"Prepare to be boarded," Undermeyer orders, maneuvering the *Check* to dock with the tanker and leaving the details for his exec to work out with its captain. So far it sounds good, but Undermeyer is a hard man to convince these days.

"Chief Perez." He stares at the massive Slug on the screen. "Take your men and a unit of my men, armed with laser rifles and gas grenades. Secure the Mayday, if that is what it is."

The chief jogs his men into the airlock, the unit of spacemen jogging behind them. They cross and board the *Last Chance*. So far it is as advertised, but there is no welcoming committee.

"Jimenez," the chief hisses. He holds up two fingers, then points his rifle down the passage to the engine room.

Jimenez detaches his squad and gestures to one of his two Slugs, a muscular, stocky woman, to take the point. She runs down the deck to the first turn and holds the corner as her buddy slams his body to the far corner. Jimenez brings up the rear, sliding around the corner, as his point moves out, followed in turn by his patrol. Then they are out of sight.

The chief points to Popolus and hisses, "Greek, engine room," holding up two fingers. The Greek takes two Slugs and jogs down the gangway to the hatch leading below.

All are in pressure suits, and all have pacifier-disrupters in place.

The pacifier is an insidious little device, first developed to render criminals pliable for trial and rehabilitation. It soon became available to the criminal syndicates and was mass-marketed to thieves and pirates throughout the system. No amount of public pressure could create the legislation that would freely supply the disrupter to honest, law-abiding citizens for self-protection. So, except for those who can afford to support the brisk black market trade in them, colonists are easy pickings for raiders.

The communications button in Perez's ear crackles.

"Engine room secure, Chief," the squad leader reports.

Seconds later, Jimenez reports in. "Cargo bay looks like a bomb hit it, Chief. The bay doors are leaking like a sieve."

"Okay, join up and move up to general quarters deck. Spaceman," he barks, addressing the leader of the regular forces, "dispatch a patrol behind my men and hold both the engine room and cargo bay."

"Yes, Chief. You, you, and you, with Hildeman. You three with Rosario. Move. The rest on me."

They move up to the bridge, leaving three men in the airlock. There are five people on the bridge: two men, a woman, and two children. (They look dirty and unkempt, except one of the men, who is dark and greasy and has beady eyes that won't meet anyone else's for long.)

"Who's in charge here?" the chief grunts, watching the greasy man and pointing his weapon in the man's general direction.

"I am." The dark man steps forward. "Thank God you are here. If you could help us repair, we will be on our way. We certainly didn't wish to cause the navy any trouble."

"Right," the chief says, but in his mind he screams *Wrong*. These people are hostages, and their captors didn't expect to attract a fleet. The details of how the "leak" is controlled or how long they have been holding these people as bait are not clear, but what *is* clear is that there are a lot of very nasty pirates around somewhere.

"Chief, Hildeman. They've breached . . ."

"Shit!" the chief bellows, taking out the dark man with a burst from his laser rifle. "Hold these people. Secure the bridge." The regular forces take the bridge as the chief and six Slugs are bounding triple time toward the cargo bay.

"We are under attack," he radios the *Check*. Shouting orders to his two patrols as he runs, he and his men hit the doors of the cargo bay. The bay is filled with pirates.

Ships' Marines (Slugs)

Manpower 7
Ordnance 9
Melee 9

Stealth 5
Morale (same as fleet)

There are 7 Slugs in the bay, each heavily armed. Slugs have a Melee Value of 9 each. Their total Attack Strength is therefore 63 to start the attack.

Pirates

Manpower 21
Ordnance 2
Melee 2
Stealth 2
Morale 5

There are 21 pirates. They are variously armed, with average ordnance, and have a Melee Value of 2 apiece. They are not trained as a unit and are getting in each other's way, but they have the numbers and the position.

The Slugs fire from Chart B, the pirates using Chart E.

If the Slugs kill all the pirates, turn to section 37.

If the pirates overcome the Slugs, turn to section 38.

— 17 —

The chief slams his body against the bay door for cover, shooting short bursts at the ragged mass of pirates, whose vacuum suits appear hardly able to hold air.

"Jimenez, Greek, to the cargo bay," he shouts into his helmet mike.

But it will take time for reinforcements, he realizes, and this could be over in seconds. The Slugs are good, but the numbers are not with them.

"Die, sucker," a Slug bellows as she burns the guts out of a pirate.

"How'd they get in?" a kid shouts.

"Hid on the hull. Assholes on deck didn't see them. We walked right into this."

"Shit," the woman spits, as she drops an empty clip and reaches for a new one. A burly black man rushes her with a savage growl. She brings the butt of her rifle up sharply, crushing his jaw, and follows up with a jab to his windpipe. When her clip is in place, she finishes the job.

"Needle-heads!" she shouts to her comrades.

The pirates fight with an insanity and courage that comes out of a syringe. That makes them both easy to kill and dangerous. They don't fight with skill or brains, but they are damned hard to stop.

Finally it is over. The cargo bay looks like a slaughterhouse, the deck slick with blood and piled with bodies. The chief pokes his rifle at the last man he has shot, but the pirate is as dead as his comrades.

"Shee-it!" he mutters as he calls roll to assess his own losses. There are a lot of unanswered names. By now the rest of his men and the surviving regulars who were not posted come charging in.

The ship is secure and the civilian hostages are rounded up, under guard just in case. But the airlock is sealed and the *Check* gone.

Turn to section 20.

— 18 —

The chief slams his body against the bay door for cover, shooting short bursts at the ragged mass of men, their vacuum suits looking hardly able to hold air.

"Jimenez, Greek, to the cargo bay," he shouts into his helmet mike.

But it will take time for reinforcements, and this could be over in seconds. The Slugs are good, but the numbers are not with them.

"Die, sucker," a Slug bellows as she burns the guts out of a pirate.

"How'd they get in?" a kid shouts.

"Hid on the hull. Assholes on deck didn't see them. We walked right into this."

"Shit," the woman spits, as she drops an empty clip and

reaches for a new one. A burly black man rushes her with a savage growl. She brings the butt of her rifle up sharply, crushing his jaw, and follows up with a jab to his windpipe. When her clip is in place she finishes the job.

"Needle-heads!" she shouts to her comrades.

The pirates fight with an insanity and courage that comes out of a syringe. That makes them both easy to kill and dangerous. They don't fight with skill or brains, but they are damned hard to stop.

When it is over, the cargo bay looks like a slaughterhouse, the deck slick with blood and piled with bodies as the chief orders a retreat from the bay. Firepower and training are just no match against the mass of drugged criminals. The pirates cut down the remaining Slugs.

It is grim and mean reinforcements that come firing down the deck. The remaining six Slugs and three regulars charge into range.

The navy forces attack with an initial Attack Strength of 66 and fire using Chart B. The remaining pirates fire from Chart E.

If no pirates remain alive after this battle, turn to section 19.

If the pirates wipe out the entire naval force (assume that the remaining naval personnel posted are ambushed and killed), turn to section 21.

— 19 —

The naval forces have the position now, firing from cover at the hatch leading to the upper deck. The tide has turned. The drug of anger is stronger than the bottled courage of the pirates.

"Die, you bloody bastard," sobs the ranking surviving enlisted man as he blasts the head off the last pirate.

"Shee-it!" he mutters. When he calls roll to assess his own losses, there are many unanswered names.

The ship is secure, and the civilian hostages are rounded

up, under guard just in case. But the airlock is sealed and the *Check* gone.

Turn to section 20.

— 20 —

Undermeyer paces while the story from the *Chance* unfolds through disjointed dialogue from the intercom and fuzzy pictures from the console. But just as Chief Perez is about to walk into the tanker's cargo bay, the captain is told that he has troubles of his own. A state-of-the-art torpedo has been launched at the *Pike*. They watch helplessly as she is destroyed.

"What the hell? Where did that come from? Battle stations. Seal off that hatch."

In the ordered frenzy of space battles, the *Check* comes about, and the captain assumes command of his force. The pirate lure was more sinister than it looked. The drug-crazed berserkers were as much a diversion as the hostages. The real threat is a very modern and well-appointed destroyer with two escort vessels.

Cross off the Pike *on your Ship Loss Record Sheet.*

The navy's 4 ships have an Ordnance Value of 7 each. They attack using Chart C.

The pirates' 3 ships have an Ordnance Value of 8 each. They fire from Chart E.

If any of the four USJ ships survive, subtract any losses from the Ship Loss Record sheet and turn to section 23.

If the navy does not survive, subtract the remaining 4 vessels from the Ship Loss Record Sheet and turn to section 24.

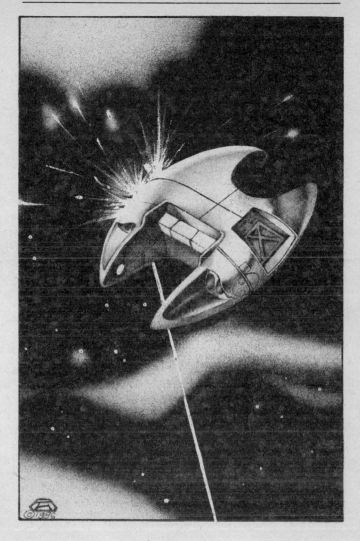

— 21 —

Once again the trained and armed men are felled by the rabble. Triumphant, the tattered remains of the crazed pirate band head for the airlock to take on the navy ship. The frenzy of drug-induced courage gleams in their eyes.

But the airlock is sealed and the destroyer is gone.

Turn to section 22.

— 22 —

Undermeyer paces while the story from the *Chance* unfolds through disjointed dialogue from the intercom and fuzzy pictures from the console. But just as Chief Perez is about to walk into the tanker's cargo bay, the captain is told that he has troubles of his own. A state-of-the-art torpedo has been launched at the *Pike*. They watch helplessly as she is destroyed.

"What the hell? Where did that come from? Battle stations. Seal off that hatch."

In the ordered frenzy of space battles, the *Check* comes about, and the captain assumes command of his force. The pirate lure was more sinister than it looked. The drug-crazed berserkers were as much a diversion as the hostages. The real threat is a very modern and well-appointed destroyer with two escort vessels.

Remove the Pike *from your Ship Loss Record Sheet.*

The 4 navy ships have an Ordnance Value of 7 each, and fire using Chart C.

The 3 pirate vessels have an Ordnance Value of 8 each, and fire from Chart D.

If the navy survives, subtract any ships lost from the Ship Loss Record Sheet and go to section 25.

If all 4 USJ ships are destroyed, subtract the 4 remaining ships lost and go to section 26.

— 23 —

The last enemy vessel disappears into a satisfying pattern of rubble, the result of a direct torpedo hit on its engines.

"Sir, the party aboard the *Chance* is on the line. Can they be brought on board, sir?"

"Yes, spaceman. Reel them in."

The bloodied survivors of the boarding party rejoin the bloodied survivors of the space battle. The hostages are comfortably but firmly confined to quarters pending serious debriefing, and the wing begins its long chase back to the fleet.

Go to section 27.

— 24 —

The survivors aboard the *Last Chance* follow the battle from the bridge. Their fate unfolds as blips on the screen wink out, marking the death of their buddies.

"Damn them," the ranking officer sobs. "Mine this damn ship. Use grenades, and all the ammo. We're not going alone."

They wait until they hear the pirate ship dock. Then the CO pulls the pin.

In the dark of space, a momentary brilliance marks the memorial to a few brave men and women.

Go to section 28.

— 25 —

The last enemy vessel disappears into a satisfying pattern of rubble, the result of a direct torpedo hit on the engines.

"Sir, we're getting a faint signal from the party aboard the *Chance*. I'll try to boost it. Can they be brought on board, sir?"

"Yes, spaceman. Reel them in."

"Sir, you'd better hear this first." The communication tech puts the line on an open channel.

A screaming man's voice fills the bridge. "We killed them. We killed them all. We will kill you this life or the next."

The captain quickly takes stock of the situation. There are no naval personnel left, and no hostages.

"Nuke them," he orders, staring stiffly ahead.

"Stand ready. Fire laser cannons on my mark. Fire."

The commands are a wrathful memorial to the buddies who will never come home. The tattered wing begins its long flight back to the fleet.

Turn to section 27.

— 26 —

The remaining battle- and drug-mad pirates murder the hostages, and are picked up by their comrades. The pirate destroyer heads for a secret rendezvous. Its captain is not as insane as the beasts he keeps for hand-to-hand combat. He has no desire to take on the entire Jupe navy alone.

Turn to section 28.

— 27 —

"Commander, something is wrong."

The fleet has been hauling ass the whole time the wing was out on the rescue mission, and they were, as was to be expected, running late.

Emerald stares at the place on the screen where Dixon is pointing. Some of the blips are, well . . . shimmering is the way it looks. No, they are separating. Something or someone has been hiding behind space debris and is now making a move.

"It was a trap. A damn trap." She briefly considers long-range communication in defiance of her own command, but it would be a futile and dangerous move. Besides, in the few seconds they have been watching, the battle is already engaged.

She watches, trying to keep track of Ours and Theirs from the faint moving smudges on the screen.

After a long time, there is a movement of blips back toward the fleet, clearly Ours.

She orders the fleet to slow, once more biting into precious time.

After two more hours the wing rejoins the fleet but they don't bring unequivocal victory. Emerald assesses her losses. She has lost a total of two more hours, and they are not even halfway to the ford.

Subtract 2 hours from your time chart.

Turn to section 30.

— 28 —

"Commander, something is wrong."

The fleet has been hauling ass the whole time the wing was out on the rescue mission, and they were, as was to be expected, running late.

Emerald stares at the place on the screen where Dixon is pointing. Some of the blips are, well . . . shimmering is the way it looks. No, they are separating. Something or someone has been hiding behind space debris and is now making a move.

"It was a trap. A damn trap." She briefly considers long-range communication in defiance of her own command, but it would be a futile and dangerous move. Besides, in the few seconds they have been watching, the battle is already engaged.

She watches, trying to keep track of Ours and Theirs from the faint moving smudges on the screen.

After a long time, there is a clear movement of blips away from the fleet. She has lost more men, and more ships, including the fastest and best destroyer in the navy. This was not the best battle she had fought.

Subtract ½ hour from your time chart.

Turn to section 30.

— 29 —

The first thing a soldier has to do is stay alive. Heroics don't help if you're dead when you are needed. The next thing a soldier has to do is obey orders. Take a hill. Hold a bridge. Everything else is extra. The extras get you medals, or court-martialed, but they usually don't win wars.

Bad luck? Bad tactics? It doesn't matter. If Emerald had made her rendezvous, the result would have been a rout of the enemy, a victory for the task force. But this time she failed.

Would you like to try again? If so, go to section 1. If you think you got a rotten break, treat yourself to two extra escort ships (the Catherine *and the* Penny*) next time around. Good luck!*

— 30 —

One thing was clear from this last encounter: the flotilla was not crossing unoccupied space. Emerald knows that if this were her territory, she would be patrolling both sides of the Danube and the Sajo, and any other "territorial cover," to use a terrestrial analogy. And, despite the chatter that the pirates were illiterate oafs, she knows that you don't get to hold vast wealth and power by being stupid. She also knows that if she were the enemy she would have deployed recon up the wazoo, given that the naval task force has been on a successful pirate hunt for years.

It is time to do some heavy scouting. She, of course, has deployed some of the faster, smaller vessels on point, and they have been relaying back map and intelligence information. What she needs to do now is to drop the speed of the convoy and send recon parties out on a serious sweep. Something is going on out there in a very organized way.

The bird class escorts were the closest thing the modern navy had to dogfighters, not counting the drones, although the analogy was not perfect. The birds also had some features of the ancient, low-altitude bombers and intelligence ships. They could strafe into most atmospheres, being light and well shielded, and their stealth was about ten on a scale of one to twelve. And they could haul a classified 5.2 gee or better, given the crazies who flew them.

"Let's fly some birds. Give me the duty roster. I want Preacher, Kiwi, and, let's see . . ."

"How about Weasel? I used to date him. He's tops. No, honest, he's good," Dixon finishes lamely.

"Okay, Weasel. Scramble them. Remind them this is recon. Don't fire unless fired on, and then only if they can't run."

The three birds are loosed and begin a grid search. Within an hour, they have made contact.

"Good jumping Jeez, Weasel," the range intercept officer half whispers to his pilot. "Lookie there."

Weasel looks to his right and sees emerging from the fog of

space dust a fleet: two cruisers, two destroyers, and six escorts.

"Let's book, rook," he orders his rookie RIO, call sign the Rabbit. "It's afterburner city!" Weasel shouts, wheeling the craft in a move the engineers who designed it never dreamed about except in nightmares.

"We're hoppin', we're hoppin' now!" hoots the Rabbit.

The other birds have found the enemy, too, and are in range of the massive cruiser. It's time to run home to Mother Hen.

Subtract ½ hour for the reduced speed of the task force fleet.

Roll two six-sided dice. If the total rolled is the same as or less than the Stealth Value of the bird recon ships, which is 10, turn to section 31.

If the total is greater, turn to section 32.

Initial enemy strength:

Type	Ordnance
Cruiser 1	12*
Cruiser 2	12*
Destroyer 1	6
Destroyer 2	6
Escort 1	6
Escort 2	6
Escort 3	6
Escort 4	6
Escort 5	6
Escort 6	6

*Treat as 2 Ordnance 6 ships when computing the pirates' attack value.

— 31 —

As soon as the first bird is in safe transmission range, the pilot contacts his base.

"Weasel to Mother Hen, over."

"Mother Hen, over."

"We are boogying to the coop with a fleet on our ass. Transmitting all data, on your signal."

"We copy. Begin transmission on my mark. Mark."

Emerald has just gulped down something that passes in the navy for a ham and cheese sandwich, and swallowed her second pack of cola this hour, when the report comes in.

Her eyes glimmering with concentration, she takes stock of her fleet and checks her wrist chronometer. Is there any way out of a full-scale space battle? They can't pull off an end run. It's not like kickball. It takes time to move a couple of dozen warships, time they don't have. They can't possibly sneak past the enemy, although they are sure going to try. *This is it, girl,* she thinks. *If you've got it, use it.*

"Battle stations. Battle stations," the intercom wails.

Men dive into vacuum suits and fire gear, the sound of boots ringing throughout the flotilla as everyone hits the deck racing to their posts, preparing ammo, laser packs, and the thousand things that stand in readiness but need to be looked at once more.

Emerald is quivering like a racehorse at the gate as they approach the position where the enemy fleet lies.

They are running silent, allowing for no detection device to reveal their position. Emerald does not doubt for one second that their presence is known or that the enemy commander is not fully aware that the navy knows his own position.

"Contact, ma'am," the EIO whispers.

The navy fleet drifts on, waiting.

For one hysterical moment, Emerald thinks that they will make it through. They are risking attack from the flank with each successive moment, although they have oriented as much lateral firepower as possible along the right flank, the side on which the enemy is poised.

"Enemy torpedo, incoming!"

The Klaxons wail. The ship swerves to avoid the torpedo, its frame shuddering dangerously, but the torpedo misses, shooting past the fleet to detonate on an asteroid somewhere beyond.

Turn to section 33.

— 32 —

Two of the three birds are fired on only once each. The third is able to escape unscathed. The enemy fires at each of the birds with an Attack Strength of 20 (potshots, not an organized attack) using Chart E. The birds are so badly outnumbered that they do not return fire, but escape if they can. If the enemy destroys any of the birds, subtract it from the fleet total on the Ship Loss Record Sheet.

Turn to section 31.

— 33 —

Remember the Brooksville, *the cruiser stranded for repairs? Ever wonder what happened to her? Roll two six-sided dice.*

If the total is the same or less than the fleet value for Morale, turn to section 34.

If the total is greater than the value for Morale, turn to section 35.

— 34 —

Suddenly, out of nowhere, the starburst of a direct hit fills the screen and momentarily blacks out the radar screen.

"What the hell was that?"

"Someone on our side, I'd guess," Emerald observes dryly.

"*Brooksville* to *Inverness*. Permission to return to the line."

"Permission granted," Emerald shouts. A lot of objects are happily thrown into the air.

The *Brooksville* has taken out one of the enemy cruisers, but the battle is now on.

Add the Brooksville *to the task force fleet.*

Subtract 1 cruiser from the enemy fleet, bringing them down to 9 ships.

Turn to section 36.

— 35 —

Somewhere out in space the crew of the *Brooksville* tries to find the problem in their engines. When they finally do track it down, they find that the complete CT drive is fused. Nothing short of a major repair facility will help. They fire up their auxiliary engines, hoping, at least, to be able to return to the main fleet.

Turn to section 54.

— 36 —

"Okay, folks," Emerald says, gathering her staff. She leans over the console, supported by her elbows, her face lit from below by the eerie green of the screen.

Dixon is tapping out lists of stats on the surviving ships of the line. Ammo, fuel, manpower. And the status of the secret weapon.

It was Emerald's brainstorm. Who said you have to fly drones from a carrier? Their souped-up little tugs have been bravely towing a small fleet of the unmanned fighters; three each for a total of nine. This is Sheller's ace in the hole. The controls on board the *Inverness* are all operational. The flight crew is ready for remote launch and deployment.

"What have we got? Let's review. Dixon, your show."

Dixon lists all the ships available for combat, grouping

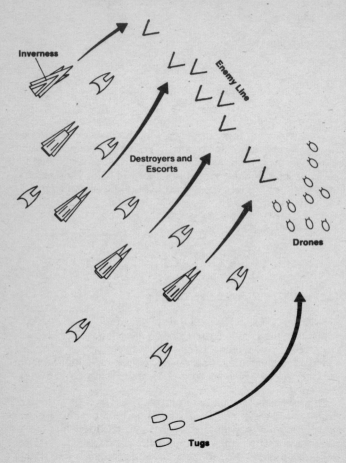

CONFIGURATION FOR FULL-SCALE ATTACK

Inverness

Enemy Line

Destroyers and Escorts

Drones

Tugs

TACTICS OF HOLDING FORCE

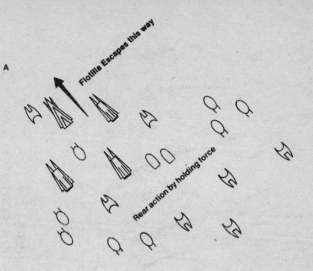

A

Flotilla Escapes this way

Rear action by holding force

B **Swarm Tactics**

Concentrated Navy fire on single target

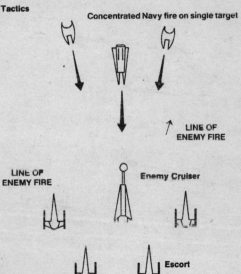

↑ LINE OF
ENEMY FIRE

↑ LINE OF
ENEMY FIRE

Enemy Cruiser

Escort

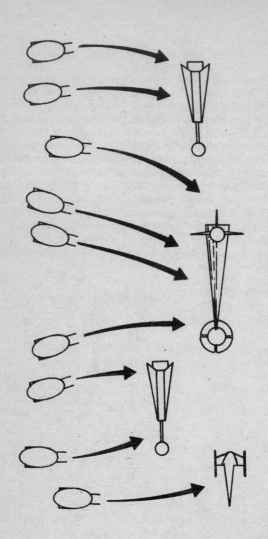

DRONE STRIKE—MASS FIRE ON ENEMY FLAGSHIP AND ESCORT

them by class: cruisers, destroyers, the various sorts of escort vessels (which she lumped in one category: fast and light), and the tugs-cum-drones.

"Good. The sum of this status report is that we are running at about seventy percent efficiency," Emerald announces, her stylus bringing up more charts and figures on her screen.

"We have several choices," Emerald states. "We can hit them with everything we've got. This gives us the best numerical advantage, but we risk a time and matériel factor. Remember, people, the objective is to rendezvous with the main fleet at the Sajo pass.

"Our second option is to deploy a smaller, suicide squad. If they can hold the enemy long enough, we could get through with the flotilla. Risk: If they fail, we will still have a stand-up fight with the enemy, and with a weaker force at our disposal.

"Third option. We go with the drones in a first strike. We test their firepower, and inflict some damage. Then we decide to hit or run, given our success and their casualties."

These three battle plans are presented on Maps 3, 4, and 5. Which will you choose?

If you opt for a full-scale attack, turn to section 53.

If you opt for a holding action, turn to section 55.

If you opt for a strike by the drones, turn to section 56.

Initial enemy strength:

Type	Ordnance
Cruiser 1	12*
Cruiser 2	12*
Destroyer 1	6
Destroyer 2	6
Escort 1	6
Escort 2	6
Escort 3	6
Escort 4	6
Escort 5	6
Escort 6	6

*Treat as 2 Ordnance 6 ships when computing attack values.

— 37 —

The chief slams his body against the bay door for cover, shooting short bursts at the ragged mass of pirates, whose vacuum suits appear hardly able to hold air.

"Jimenez, Greek, to the cargo bay," he shouts into his helmet-mike.

But it will take time for reinforcements, he realizes, and this could be over in seconds. The Slugs are good, but the numbers are not with them.

"Die, sucker," a Slug bellows as she burns the guts out of a pirate.

"How'd they get in?" a kid shouts.

"Hid on the hull. Assholes on deck didn't see them. We walked right into this."

"Shit," the woman spits, as she drops an empty clip and searches for a new one. A burly black man rushes her, with a savage growl. She brings the butt of her rifle up sharply, crushing his jaw, and follows through with a jab to his windpipe. When her clip is in place she finishes the job.

"Needle-heads!" she shouts to her comrades.

The pirates fight with an insanity and courage that comes out of a syringe. That makes them both easy to kill and dangerous. They don't fight with skill or brains, but they are damned hard to stop.

Finally it is over. The cargo bay looks like a slaughter-house, the deck slick with blood and piled with bodies. The chief pokes his rifle at the last man he has shot, but the pirate is as dead as his comrades.

"Shee-it!" the chief mutters as he calls roll to assess his own losses. A lot of names go unanswered. By now, the rest of his men and the surviving regulars who are not posted come charging in.

The ship is secure and the civilian hostages are rounded up, under guard just in case. But the airlock is sealed and the *Check* gone.

Turn to section 40.

— 38 —

The chief slams his body against the bay door for cover, shooting short bursts at the ragged mass of pirates, whose vacuum suits appear hardly able to hold air.

"Jimenez, Greek, to the cargo bay," he shouts into his helmet-mike.

But it will take time for reinforcements, he realizes, and this could be over in seconds. The Slugs are good, but the numbers are not with them.

"Die, sucker," a Slug bellows as she burns the guts out of a pirate.

"How'd they get in?" a kid shouts.

"Hid on the hull. Assholes on deck didn't see them. We walked right into this."

"Shit," the woman spits, as she drops an empty clip and reaches for a new one. A burly black man rushes her with a savage growl. She brings the butt of her rifle up sharply, crushing his jaw, and follows through with a jab to his windpipe. When her clip is in place she finishes the job.

"Needle-heads!" she shouts to her comrades.

The pirates fight with an insanity and courage that comes out of a syringe. That makes them both easy to kill and dangerous. They don't fight with skill or brains, but they are damned hard to stop.

The cargo bay looks like a slaughterhouse, the deck slick with blood and piled with bodies, as the chief orders a retreat from the bay. The firepower and training are just no match against the mass of drugged criminals. The pirates cut down the remaining Slugs as they retreat.

It is grim and mean reinforcements that come firing down the deck. The remaining six Slugs and three regulars charge into range.

The navy forces attack with an initial Manpower Value of 9 and an Ordnance Value of 9, and fire using Chart C. The remaining pirates fire from Chart F.

If no pirates remain alive after this battle, turn to section 39.

If the pirates wipe out the entire naval force (assume that the remaining naval personnel not in the battle are unarmed, unable to leave their stations, and killed), turn to section 41.

— 39 —

The naval forces have the position now, firing from cover at the hatch leading to the upper deck. The tide has turned. The drug of anger is stronger than the bottled courage of the pirates.

"Die, you bloody bastard," sobs the ranking surviving enlisted man as he blasts the head off the last pirate.

"Shee-it!" he groans as he calls roll to assess his own losses. A lot of names go unanswered.

The ship is secure, and the civilian hostages are rounded up, under guard just in case. But the airlock is sealed and the *Check* gone.

Turn to section 40.

— 40 —

Undermeyer paces while the story from the *Last Chance* unfolds through disjointed dialogue from the intercom and fuzzy pictures from the console. But just as Chief Perez is about to walk into the tanker's cargo bay, the captain is told that he has troubles of his own. A state-of-the-art torpedo has been launched at the *Pike*. They watch helplessly as she is destroyed.

"What the hell? Where did that come from? Battle stations. Seal off that hatch."

In the ordered frenzy of space battles, the *Check* comes about, and the captain assumes command of his force. The pirate lure was more sinister than it looked. The drug-crazed berserkers were as much a diversion as the hostages. The real threat is a very modern and well-appointed destroyer with two escort vessels.

Remove the Pike *from the Ship Loss Record Sheet.*

The 4 navy ships have an Ordnance of 7 each, and attack using Chart C.

The 3 pirate vessels each have an Ordnance of 8, and attack using Chart E.

If the navy survives, subtract any losses on the Ship Loss Record Sheet and turn to section 43.

If all 4 USJ vessels are lost, cross them off on the Ship Loss Record Sheet and turn to section 44.

— 41 —

Once again, the trained and armed men are felled by the rabble. Triumphant, the tattered remains of the crazed pirate band head for the airlock to take on the navy ship. The frenzy of drug-induced courage gleams in their eyes.
But the airlock is sealed, and the destroyer is gone.

Turn to section 42.

— 42 —

Undermeyer paces as the story from the *Last Chance* unfolds through disjointed dialogue from the intercom and fuzzy pictures from the console. But just as Chief Perez is about to walk into the tanker's cargo bay, the captain is told that he has troubles of his own. A state-of-the-art torpedo has been launched at the *Pike*. They watch helplessly as she is destroyed.
"What the hell? Where did that come from? Battle stations. Seal off that hatch."
In the ordered frenzy of space battles, the *Check* comes about, and the captain assumes command of his force. The pirate lure was more sinister than it looked. The drug-crazed

berserkers were as much a diversion as the hostages. The real threat is a very modern and well-appointed destroyer with two escort vessels.

Remove the Pike *from the Record Sheet.*

The 4 navy ships each have an Ordnance of 7, and attack using Chart C.

The 3 pirate vessels each have an Ordnance of 8, and attack using Chart E.

If the navy survives, subtract any losses on the Ship Loss Record Sheet and turn to section 45.

If all 4 USJ vessels are lost, cross them off on the Ship Loss Record Sheet and turn to section 46.

— 43 —

The last enemy vessel disappears into a satisfying pattern of rubble, the result of a direct torpedo hit on its engines.

"Sir, the party aboard the *Chance* is on the line. Can they be brought on board, sir?"

"Yes, spaceman. Reel them in."

The bloodied survivors of the boarding party rejoin the bloody survivors of the space battle. The hostages are comfortably but firmly confined to quarters pending serious debriefing, and the wing begins its long chase back to the fleet.

Go to section 47.

— 44 —

The survivors aboard the *Last Chance* follow the battle from the bridge. Their fate unfolds as blips on the screen wink out, marking the doom of their buddies and themselves.

"Damn them," the CO sobs. "Mine the damn ship. Use the grenades and the rest of the ammo. We're not going alone."

They wait until they hear the pirate ship dock. Then the CO pulls the pin.

In the dark of space, a momentary brilliance marks the memorial to a few brave men and women.

Go to section 48.

— 45 —

The last enemy vessel disappears into a satisfying pattern of rubble, the result of a direct torpedo hit on its engines.

"Sir, the party aboard the *Chance* is on the line. Can they be brought on board, sir?"

"Yes, spaceman. Reel them in."

"Sir, you'd better hear this first." The communication tech puts the line on an open channel.

A screaming man's voice fills the bridge. "We killed them. We killed them all. We will kill you this life or the next."

The captain quickly takes stock of the situation. There are no naval personnel left aboard the tanker, and no hostages.

"Nuke them," he orders, staring straight ahead. "Stand ready. Fire laser cannons on my mark. Fire."

The commands are a wrathful memorial to the buddies who will never come home. The tattered wing begins its long trek back to the fleet.

Turn to section 47.

— 46 —

The remaining battle- and drug-mad pirates murder the hostages, and are picked up by their comrades. The pirate destroyer heads for a secret rendezvous. Its captain is not as insane as the beasts he keeps for hand-to-hand combat. He has no desire to take on the entire Jupe navy alone.

Turn to section 48.

— **47** —

"Commander, something is wrong."

The fleet has been hauling ass the whole time the wing was out on the rescue mission and they were, as was to be expected, running late.

Emerald stares at the place on the screen where Dixon is pointing.

"Here, ma'am. There are some blips which are, well . . . shimmering is the way it looks. No, now they're separating."

Emerald looks puzzled for a moment, then says, in a pinched, hollow voice, "Something or someone has been hiding behind space debris and is now making a move."

The sharp little slaps as she punches her left fist into her right palm make her aide jump. It is a hard-eyed and angry Emerald who mutters, "It was a trap. A damned trap." She briefly considers long-range communication in defiance of her own command, but it would be a futile and dangerous move. Besides, in the few seconds they have been watching, the battle is already engaged.

She watches, trying to keep track of Ours and Theirs from the faint moving smudges on the screen.

After a long time, there is a movement of blips back toward the fleet, clearly Ours.

She orders the fleet to slow, once more biting into precious time.

After two more hours, the wing rejoins the fleet, but they don't bring unequivocal victory. Emerald assesses her losses. She has lost a total of two more hours, and they are not even halfway to the ford.

Subtract 2 hours from your chart.

Turn to section 50.

— 48 —

"Commander, something is wrong."

The fleet has been hauling ass the whole time the wing was out on the rescue mission, and they were, as was to be expected, running late.

Emerald stares at the place on the screen where Dixon is pointing.

"Here, ma'am. There are some blips which are, well . . . shimmering is the way it looks. No, now they're separating."

Emerald looks puzzled for a moment, then says, in a pinched, hollow voice, "Something or someone has been hiding behind space debris and is now making a move."

The sharp little slaps as she punches her left fist into her right palm make her aide jump. It is a hard-eyed and angry Emerald who mutters, "It was a trap. A damned trap." She briefly considers long-range communication in defiance of her own command, but it would be a futile and dangerous move. Besides, in the few seconds they have been watching, the battle is already engaged.

She watches, trying to keep track of Ours and Theirs from the faint moving smudges on the screen.

After a long time, there is a movement of blips away from the fleet—Theirs. She has lost more men, and more ships, including the fastest and best destroyer in the navy.

Turn to section 50.

— 49 —

The fiftyish, short, and slightly pudgy Commander Paolo Marchese paces back and forth, as they begin the course change, lurching with the blasts of attitude rockets, but refusing to sit down.

"Sparks, let's see if those geeks have our code. Send a message to the squad to move into a V configuration. Listen for enemy radio chatter. I want to know if the pirates say anything to indicate that they've picked up the command.''

"Radar, tell me if they start to respond before they have visual verification of what we're up to.''

Marchese had been passed over for promotion time and again, but he wouldn't take early retirement. The navy was his life. He had fought hard to go to OCS and had put up with more than thirty years of biased bullshit from men whose genes made them a little taller and a little thinner, and who hadn't been brought up on the back streets of New Detroit. He had won a small following among war-gamers for his analysis of the battles in Solar War I and was probably the foremost expert on the ancient Roman army.

But that and fifty cents didn't buy a cup of coffee any more. The Hubris rat pack had given him a chance, a promotion, and now a wing command.

"Sir, there is no apparent response from the enemy. They seem to be jockeying to hit the *Inverness*.''

"Bad. Code to *Golden State*. Hit them with suppressing fire from the midships turrent. To escorts: fire from nose guns at targets of opportunity, if they get any. Course adjustment: spin us back around to clear our torpedo launchers. We're going to barrel past them sideways and loose two fish. On my mark, fire. Mark!''

Two smart fish burst from the torpedo tubes and lock onto the enemy flagship, as short bursts from the ship's 30-mm guns fan out death at the enemy. The blaze from the front-mounted laser cannon on a destroyer escort scores a direct hit to one of the enemy escorts.

Meanwhile, Emerald's convoy slips gracefully past the enemy and glides on toward the mission objective. The coded messages race back and forth from Commander Marchese's command post to the bridges of his wing.

Forming a wedge, to cover the rear of Emerald's escaping flotilla, Marchese isolates one of the destroyers which is blocking the return fire on its own escorts. They hit it hard, and it explodes into space junk.

"Pull back,'' he orders, and the small band circles wide of the enemy, putting on all the speed they have and regrouping on a cruiser.

What Marchese is able to do is establish local superiority. While his total initial firepower was inferior to the firepower of the enemy wing, at any point of engagement he outguns them by hitting an isolated target without opening himself to support fire from other enemy vessels.

The tactic is good. He whips their ass.

"That's it, sir," his exec announces, fighting to keep the excitement out of her voice. "Rejoin Commander Sheller?"

"No, Greenbaum. Whatever we've got left stays here, on patrol."

Aboard the *Inverness*, Emerald hovers over a big radar screen with her staff.

The officers and enlisted men cheer as the first enemy blip disappears.

"Go, go, go," Dixon chants.

"Good move," Jackson, the youngest of the staff, mutters, fascinated by the audacity and brilliance of Marchese's deployment.

As the final enemy blip disappears, the entire bridge crew whoops and whistles.

"Yahoo!" Emerald belts out with the best of them, but as she wipes the sweat from her eyes, she sounds off crisply, "All right, you guys. Back to work."

They have lost no time and they all feel much safer with Marchese patrolling their rear.

Go to section 62.

— 50 —

One thing was clear from this last encounter: the flotilla was not crossing unoccupied space. Emerald knows that if this were her territory, she would be patrolling both sides of the Danube and the Sajo, and any other "territorial cover," to use a terrestrial analogy. And, despite the chatter that the pirates were illiterate oafs, she knows that you don't get to hold vast wealth and power by being stupid. She also knows that if she were the enemy she would have deployed recon up the wazoo, given that her task force has been on a successful pirate hunt for years.

It is time to do some heavy scouting. She, of course, had deployed some of the faster, smaller vessels on point, and they had relayed back map and intelligence information. But what she needs to do now is to drop speed and send recon parties out on a serious sweep. Something is going on out there in a very organized way.

The bird-class escorts were the closest thing the modern navy had to dogfighters, not counting the drones, although they actually were more akin to the ancient low-altitude bombers and intelligence ships. They could strafe into most atmospheres, being light and well shielded, and their stealth was about ten on a scale of one to twelve. And they could haul a classified 5.2 gee, or better, given the crazies who flew them.

"Let's fly some birds. Let's see the duty roster. Okay, Preacher, Kiwi, and, let's see . . ."

"How about Weasel? I used to date him. He's tops. No, honest, he's good," Dixon finished lamely.

"Okay, Weasel. Scramble them. Recon. Don't fire unless fired on, and then only if you can't run."

The three birds are loosed and begin a grid search. Within two hours they have made contact.

"Good jumping Jeez, Weasel," the range intercept officer half whispers to his pilot. "Lookie there."

Emerging from the fog of space dust they sight a fleet; two cruisers, two destroyers, and six escorts.

"Let's book, rook," he orders his rookie RIO, call sign the Rabbit. "It's afterburner city!" Weasel shouts, wheeling the craft in a move the engineers who designed it never dreamed about except in nightmares.

"We're hoppin', we're hoppin' now!" hoots the Rabbit.

The other birds have found them too, and are in range of the massive cruiser. It is time to run home to Mother Hen.

Subtract ½ hour for the reduced speed of the fleet.

Roll two six-sided dice. If the total is the same as or less than the Stealth of the fleet, turn to section 51.

If it is greater, turn to section 52.

Initial enemy strength:

Type	Ordnance
Cruiser 1	12*
Cruiser 2	12*

Type	Ordnance
Destroyer 1	6
Destroyer 2	6
Escort 1	6
Escort 2	6
Escort 3	6
Escort 4	6
Escort 5	6
Escort 6	6

*Treat as 2 Ordnance 6 ships when computing attack value.

— 51 —

As soon as the first bird is in safe transmission range, the pilot contacts his base.

"Weasel to Mother Hen, over."

"Mother Hen, over."

"We are boogying to the coop with a fleet on our ass. Transmitting all data, on your signal."

"We copy. Begin transmission on my mark. Mark."

Emerald has just gulped down something that passes in the navy for a ham and cheese sandwich and swallowed her second pack of cola this hour when the report comes in.

Her eyes glimmering with concentration, she takes stock of her fleet and checks her wrist chronometer. Is there any way out of a full-scale space battle? They can't pull off an end run. It's not like kickball. It takes time to move a couple of dozen warships, time they don't have. They can't possibly sneak past the enemy, although they are sure going to try. *This is it, girl*, she thinks. *If you've got it, use it.*

"Battle stations. Battle stations."

Men dive into vacuum suits and fire gear, the sound of boots ringing throughout the fleet as everyone hits the deck racing to their posts, preparing ammo, laser packs, and the thousand things that stand in readiness but need to be looked at once more.

Emerald is quivering like a racehorse at the gate as they approach the position where the enemy fleet lies.

They are running silent, allowing for no detection device to reveal their position. Emerald does not doubt for one second that their presence is known.

"Contact, ma'am," the EIO whispers.

The navy fleet drifts on, waiting.

For one hysterical moment, Emerald thinks that they will make it through. They are risking attack from the flank with each successive moment, although they have oriented as much lateral firepower as possible along the right flank.

"Enemy torpedo, incoming!"

The Klaxons wail. The ship swerves to avoid the torpedo, its frame shuddering dangerously, but the torpedo misses, shooting past the fleet to detonate on an asteroid somewhere beyond.

Suddenly, out of nowhere, the starburst of a direct hit fills the screen and momentarily blacks out the radar screen.

"What the hell was that?"

"Someone on our side, I'd guess."

"*Brooksville* to *Inverness*. Reporting the destruction of one enemy cruiser."

Amid the cheers, Emerald learns that the slower cruiser had found herself behind a drift of space dust and used the camouflage to lock on to the cruiser.

But the battle is now engaged in earnest.

Remove 1 ship from the enemy fleet.

Turn to section 36.

— 52 —

Two of the three birds are fired on only once each. The third is able to escape unscathed. The enemy fires on the birds with an Attack Strength of 20 (potshots, not an organized attack) using Chart E. The birds are so badly outnumbered that they do not return fire, but escape if they can. If any of the birds is destroyed, subtract it from the fleet total.

Turn to section 51.

— 53 —

It is quickly apparent to Emerald that her assessment of the enemy as a canny and worthy opponent is bang on.

"Those bastards knew about the Necklace," she sharply comments. "That, out there, is *their* flanking wing! We can't just stop it. We have to smash it. I'd guess that they sent maybe a third of their fleet. So the main task force will be in pretty good shape for firepower, even if we don't make the end run through the Necklace. But if even one enemy heavy cruiser gets through before our guys cross the ford, our goose is cooked. We have no choice, ladies and gentlemen, but to destroy them."

Emerald is at her finest in this sort of battle. The chips are down, but she still gets to deal at least half the table.

"Captain, I want the *Inverness* to move to a position in the van of the fleet, but as far left as possible. This will give us some protection, but we can still pin the flank."

"Dixon, do you know the infantry tactic called 'Hammer and Anvil'?"

"Yes, ma'am. Pin one flank and roll the other. The *Inverness* is the anvil, correct?"

"Correct. String the big guns, destroyers and larger, along the right. We'll be approaching diagonally, so the faster ships will have to put on some speed to make the wheel left. Deploy lighter escorts with each larger ship. They have the speed to move to the front, unload, and drop back through the holes while the heavier ships give fire to cover them. We'll fire in volleys, like the ancient infantry squares; first the escorts fire, then they drop back, then heavy fire and torpedoes from the heavy ships. If the enemy moves in, fire at will. If they retreat, we push them. Deploy the tugs on the right end of the line. They are the hammer. Each will launch its three drones, which will be on command control from the *Inverness*. Are the drone-jocks ready? Good. We crowd them. We roll them. Then we munch them."

The two fleets move into battle position, the ships' slow and ordered drift punctuated by sparking staccato blasts of attitude rockets. It is like a stately ballet performed by steel whales.

Since you have deployed the drones you may use them to attack on the second round of the battle. To do this you treat them as being 3 Ordnance 7 ships each for 1 round of fire only, each drone having an Attack Strength of 21, or 3 times that of an escort or destroyer. You must use at least 3 drones to attack, even if others are destroyed earlier. They may attack only on the second round of the battle. Drones may be taken as losses in this battle, beginning with the second round.

The USJ fire using Chart D until the drones attack, then fire on Chart C beginning with the third round.

The Marianas fire using Chart D and will fight until the last ship is destroyed.

If Emerald loses the battle, or prevails but has fewer than her required number of ships (see Introduction, "Final Force Strength"), turn to section 29.

If the navy destroys the enemy and still has enough ships remaining to complete the mission, turn to section 59.

— **54** —

As soon as the first bird is in safe transmission range, the pilot contacts his base.

"Weasel to Mother Hen, over."

"Mother Hen, over."

"We are boogying to the coop with a fleet on our ass. Transmitting all data, on your signal."

"We copy. Beginning transmission on my mark. Mark."

Emerald has just gulped down something that passes in the navy for a ham and cheese sandwich and swallowed her second pack of cola this hour when the report comes in.

Her eyes glimmering with concentration, she takes stock of her fleet and checks her wrist chronometer. Is there any way out of a full-scale space battle? They can't pull off an end run. It's not like kickball. It takes time to move a couple of dozen warships, time they don't have. They can't possibly sneak past the enemy, although they are sure going to try. *This is it, girl*, she thinks. *If you've got it, use it*.

"Battle stations. Battle stations."

Men and women dive into vacuum suits and fire gear, the sound of boots ringing throughout the fleet as everyone hits the deck racing to their posts, preparing ammo, laser packs, and the thousand things that stand in readiness but need to be looked at once more.

Emerald is quivering like a racehorse at the gate as they approach the position where the enemy fleet lies hidden.

They are running silent, allowing for no detection device to reveal their position. Emerald does not doubt for one second that their presence is known.

"Contact, ma'am," the EIO whispers.

The navy fleet drifts on, waiting.

For one hysterical moment Emerald thinks that they will make it through. They are risking attack from the flank with each successive moment, although they have oriented as much lateral firepower as possible along the right flank.

"Enemy torpedo, incoming!"

The Klaxons wail. The ship swerves to avoid the torpedo, its frame shuddering dangerously, but the torpedo misses, shooting past the fleet to detonate on an asteroid somewhere beyond.

But the battle is now on.

Turn to section 36.

— 55 —

It is quickly apparent to Emerald that her assessment of the enemy as a canny and worthy opponent is bang on.

"Those bastards knew about the Necklace," she comments sharply. "That, out there, is *their* flanking wing! I'd guess that they sent maybe half their fleet. So the main task force will be in pretty good shape for firepower, even if we don't make the end run through the Necklace. But if they try to hit the task force in the rear by surprise and even one heavy cruiser gets through before our guys cross the ford, our goose is cooked.

"That means we either have to smash them here or break radio silence and warn the *Sawfish*."

"But, ma'am," Lieutenant Jackson bursts out, aghast. The importance of stealth on this mission has been impressed quite firmly on everybody.

Emerald, herself, is hesitant about breaking her own order. What is the risk? There is a good chance that she can tight-beam a short message to the task force without revealing her position. Of course, if the enemy decodes it they will know that someone is poking around in an area below the Necklace, but not necessarily that a flotilla is on the way.

She considers that her primary objective is to make the end run, although the presence of so large an enemy force on her side of the Necklace might make their sneak attack, while effective, unnecessary. The whole strategy now seems unclear, and Emerald debates her tactical response to the present danger.

If she decides to refuse the attack, deploy a small holding force, and to break radio silence, turn to section 60.

If she decides to refuse the attack, deploy a small holding force, but maintain radio silence, turn to section 61.

— 56 —

It is quickly apparent to Emerald that her assessment of the enemy as a canny and worthy opponent is bang on.

"Those bastards knew about the Necklace," she comments sharply. "That, out there, is *their* flanking wing! I'd guess that they sent maybe half their fleet. So the main task force will be in pretty good shape for fire power, even if we don't make the end run through the Necklace. But if they try to hit the task force in the rear by surprise and even one heavy cruiser gets through before our guys cross the ford, our goose is cooked.

"Get on the horn to the *Sawfish*," Emerald barks out.

"But, ma'am. That would break long-range communication silence," Lieutenant Jackson protests, aghast.

"Screw radio silence! Everybody in the sector already knows we're here. We might as well have sent out invitations. Beam it tight, in code. If anything gets through the space dust to the Marianas command, it isn't going to tell them much except that we have patrol ships.

"It's a risk but it beats what's in second place. The main fleet can handle this wing if it's warned. No sweat. Our main fleet is their objective, so it's a percentage call whether they pursue or refuse attack against us. If they feel that we are the greater threat, they just might abandon their objective and hit us. If they figure they still have a chance to cause some attrition on our task force, then they'll disengage and steam on. I want them to make the first move, so let's set them up to do that. Let's test them. Show me your power, baby, show me your power," Emerald concludes, chortling over the old navy challenge. *Yeah, show me yours, sweetie, but I'm not ready to show you mine,* she thinks as she tersely punches the communications switch to the Engineering section. "Are the drones operational?"

"Yes, ma'am, and the drone-jocks plugged in."

"Let 'em rip."

The little, unassuming tugs bloom and fizzle as their attitude rockets fire in tiny puffs, changing their courses and taking them to the front line.

Seated at a radar console, much like the one aboard the *Inverness*, sits the steel-eyed pirate commander. His military bearing makes his faded gray jumpsuit look as spit-and-polish as any navy admiral's.

"What the hell are they up to?" he mutters as he stares at his printout. "Gnats attacking elephants?"

His answer comes very soon. The tugs puff and glow once more, and then burst apart like opening flowers as the drones, which have been stowed like dead cargo on their hulls, glow into a life of their own and break away.

The tugs drop back, and now the enemy cruiser is facing nine very well armed wasps.

"Fire on them, damn it. Fire at will," the pirate commander bellows, the veins in his neck throbbing with fury, his careful military bearing abandoned.

But the first volley goes to the drones. Deep in the heart of the *Inverness*, nine drone pilots sit enclosed in their command consoles, oblivious to the ship around them, entranced by the immediacy of the battle taking place in the velvet, singing silence of space.

The drones fire with an Ordnance Value of 3 times a normal ship or 21, but are destroyed by their attack. Due to the drones being controlled from other ships, the Marianas fleet will get to fire first.

They both fire using Chart C.

Roll for the exchange of fire for each side, record the damages, and then turn to section 63.

— 57 —

The fiftyish, short, and slightly pudgy Commander Paolo Marchese paces back and forth, as the wing begins a course change, lurching with the blasts of attitude rockets, but refusing to sit down.

"Sparks, let's see if those geeks have our code. Send a message to the squad to form a V configuration. Listen for radio chatter. I want to know if they say anything to indicate that they've picked up the command.

"Radar, tell me if they start to respond before they see what we're up to."

Marchese had been passed over for promotion time and again, but he wouldn't take early retirement. The navy was his life. He had fought hard to go to OCS, and had put up with more than thirty years of biased bullshit from men whose genes made them a little taller and a little thinner, and who hadn't been brought up on the back streets of New Detroit. He had won a small following among war-gamers for his analysis of the battles in Solar War I and was probably the foremost expert on the ancient Roman army.

But that and fifty cents didn't buy a cup of coffee anymore. The Hubris rat pack had given him a chance, a promotion, and now a wing command.

"Sir, there is no apparent response from the enemy. They seem to be jockeying to hit the *Inverness*."

"Bad. Code to *Golden State*. Hit them with suppressing fire from the midships turret. To escorts, fire from nose guns at targets of opportunity, if they get one. Course adjustment, spin us back to clear the torpedo launchers. We're going to barrel past them sideways. On my mark, fire. Mark!"

Two smart fish burst from the torpedo tubes and lock onto the enemy flagship, as short bursts from the ship's guns fan out death at the enemy. The blaze from the front-mounted laser cannon on a destroyer escort scores a direct hit to one of the enemy escorts.

Meanwhile, Emerald's convoy slips gracefully past the enemy and glides on to the mission objective. The coded messages race back and forth from Commander Marchese's command post to the bridges of his wing.

Forming a wedge to cover the rear of Emerald's escaping fleet, Marchese isolates one of the destroyers, which is blocking the return fire of its own escorts. They hit it hard, and it explodes into space junk.

"Pull back," he orders, and the small band circles wide of the enemy, putting on all the speed they have and regrouping on a cruiser.

What Marchese is able to do is to establish local superiority, so that while his total initial firepower was inferior to the firepower of the enemy wing, at any point of engagement he outguns them by hitting an isolated target without opening himself to support fire from other enemy vessels.

The tactic is good, but not good enough. Sometimes success in war is determined by skill, sometimes by the odds, sometimes by sheer luck.

In this case the luck is bad.

"The hull is breached. Decks two and three are sealed off."

"Fire in the engine room."

"Direct hit to Torpedo Tube One. Fire in the ammo hold. Wait, wait, it's contained. Thank God."

Klaxons scream as men drag foam hoses to quench the flames.

"Status on engine room," the captain bellows.

"No response, sir."

"Engine room to bridge. Cooling system out—"

The miniature nova of Marchese's exploding ship is felt aboard the surviving enemy ships.

It is over.

Aboard the *Inverness*, Emerald hovers around the big radar screen with her staff.

The officers and enlisted men cheer as the first enemy blip disappears.

"Go, go, go," Dixon chants.

"Good move," Lieutenant Jackson, the youngest of the staff, mutters, fascinated by the audacity and brilliance of Marchese's deployment.

But the room grows quiet as the tide turns. The wing is doing damage, but it is taking worse than it gives.

As the last naval vessel's blip fades, the crowd silently drifts away from the radar display.

Emerald's voice rings out on the bridge. "Marchese was a brilliant man, and if we survive this I'm putting him in for a Silver Star. He knew it was a suicide mission and he requested it. He bought us time. And he hurt the enemy's end-run. The task force will mop up what's left, and without taking fire, I'll bet."

Her eulogy, although a little forced, puts her people back on track as they glide toward the mouth of the passage they have dubbed the Necklace.

Turn to section 62.

— **58** —

The fiftyish, short, and slightly pudgy Commander Paolo Marchese paces back and forth as they begin the course change, lurching with the blasts of attitude rockets, but refusing to sit down.

"Sparks, let's see if those geeks have our code. Send a message to the squad to move into the V configuration. Listen for radio chatter. I want to know if they say anything to indicate that they picked up the command.

"Radar, tell me if they start to respond before they see what we're up to."

Marchese had been passed over for promotion time and again, but he wouldn't take early retirement. The navy was his life. He had fought hard to go to OCS and had put up with more than thirty years of biased bullshit from men whose genes made them a little taller and a little thinner, and who hadn't been brought up on the back streets of New Detroit. He had won a small following among war-gamers for his analysis of the battles in Solar War I, and was probably the foremost expert on the ancient Roman army.

But that and fifty cents didn't buy a cup of coffee anymore. The Hubris rat pack had given him a chance, a promotion, and now a wing command.

"Sir, there is no apparent response from the enemy. They seem to be jockeying to hit the *Inverness*."

"Bad. Code to *Golden State*. Hit them with suppressing fire from the midships turret. To escorts, fire from nose guns at targets of opportunity, if they get one. Course adjustment, spin us back to clear the torpedo launchers. We're going to barrel past them sideways and loose two fish. On my mark, fire. Mark!"

Two smart fish burst from the torpedo tubes and lock onto the enemy flagship, as short bursts from the ship's guns fan out death at the enemy. The blaze from the front-mounted laser cannon on a destroyer escort scores a direct hit to one of the enemy escorts.

Meanwhile, Emerald's convoy ships gracefully past the enemy and glides on to the objective. The coded messages race back and forth from Commander Marchese's command post to the bridges of his wing.

Forming a wedge to cover the rear of Emerald's escaping fleet, Marchese isolates one of the destroyers, which is blocking the return fire of its own escorts. They hit it hard, and it explodes into space junk.

"Pull back," he orders, and the small band circles wide of the enemy, putting on all the speed they have and regrouping on a cruiser.

What Marchese is able to do is to establish local superiority. While his total initial firepower was inferior to the firepower of the enemy wing, at any point of engagement he outguns them by hitting an isolated target without opening himself to support fire from other enemy vessels.

The tactic is good, but not good enough. Sometimes success in war is determined by skill, sometimes by the odds, sometimes by sheer luck.

In this case the luck is bad.

"The hull is breached. Decks two and three are sealed off."

"Fire in the engine room."

"Direct hit to Torpedo Tube One. Fire in the ammo hold. Wait, wait, it's contained. Thank God."

Klaxons scream as men drag foam hoses to quench the flames.

"Status on engine room," the captain bellows.

"No response, sir."

"Engine room to bridge. Cooling system out—"

The miniature nova of Marchese's exploding ship is felt aboard the surviving enemy ships.

It is over.

Aboard the *Inverness*, Emerald hovers over the big radar screen with her staff.

The officers and enlisted men cheer as the first enemy blip disappears.

"Go, go, go," Dixon chants.

"Good move," Lieutenant Jackson, the youngest of the staff, mutters, fascinated by the audacity and brilliance of Marchese's deployment.

But the mood grows quiet as the tide of battle turns. Marchese's wing is doing damage, but it is taking worse than it gives.

As the last naval vessel's blip fades, the crowd silently drifts away from the radar display.

Emerald's voice rings out on the bridge. "Marchese was a brilliant man, and if we survive this I'm putting him in for a Silver Star. He knew it was a suicide mission, and he requested it. He bought us time and he hurt the enemy's end-run. The task force will mop up what's left, and without taking fire, I'll bet."

Her eulogy, although a little forced, puts her people back on track as they glide toward the mouth of the passage they have dubbed the Necklace.

"Ma'am," Dixon says in that certain guarded voice that junior officers use when they have something touchy to tell their seniors.

Emerald nods coolly, indicating that she should continue.

"Ma'am, should we break radio silence at this point? It seems that the remnant of the enemy wing is continuing toward the main task force."

Emerald juggles the factors again in her mind. The chances that the message will be intercepted across the heavy band of space junk ahead is minimal. The remaining enemy force can only do damage if they hit by surprise. Breaking silence is a risk, but a reasonable one.

"Screw radio silence. Everybody and their pet dog in the sector already knows we're here. We might as well have sent out invitations. Beam it tight, in code. If anything gets through the space dust to the Marianas command, it isn't going to tell them much except that we have patrol ships. It's a risk but it beats what's in second place. If warned, the main fleet can handle them without taking fire. No sweat."

Quietly she looks Dixon in the eye, a touch of a smile on her lips. "Thanks, Dixon."

Then she resumes her usual frosty demeanor and sings out, "Okay. Back to work, people."

Turn to section 62.

Turn to section 62.

— 59 —

The enemy commander drops his flagship to the rear for protection but orders the rest of his big guns to the van; their objective: the USJ flagship. To him the USJ Navy seems to be stringing out the rest of its firepower fairly thinly, although he sees them begin to wheel so that they will engage his fleet in a line. He chuckles at the stupidity of the naval commander. All he has to do is realign his ships, rotating them around their own axes, and they will face the incoming naval line. And the naval rear is weak, depending on what looks to be a trio of tugs—fast tugs, but only tugs.

Aboard the *Inverness*, Emerald is ready to release her secret weapon.

"Are the drones operational?"

"Yes, sir, and the drone-jocks plugged in."

"Let 'em rip."

The little, unassuming tugs bloom and fizzle as their attitude rockets fire in tiny puffs, changing their courses and taking them to the front line.

Seated at a radar console, much like the one aboard the *Inverness*, sits the steel-eyed pirate commander. His military bearing makes his faded gray jumpsuit look as spit-and-polish as any navy admiral's. Around him other experienced members of the Marianas top crew watch silently.

"What the hell are they up to?" he mutters as he stares at his printout. "Gnats attacking elephants?"

His answer comes very soon. The tugs puff and glow once more, and then burst apart like opening flowers as the drones, which have been stowed like dead cargo on their hulls, glow into a life of their own, and break away.

The tugs drop back, and now the enemy cruiser is facing nine very well armed wasps.

"Fire on them, damn it. Fire at will," the pirate commander bellows, the veins in his neck throbbing with fury.

But the first volley doesn't stop all the drones. Deep in the heart of the *Inverness*, drone pilots sit enclosed in their command consoles, oblivious to the ship around them, entranced by the immediacy of the battle taking place in the velvet, singing silence of space. Before each is a representation of space as seen by his drone, the three-dimensional screen ahead of them outlining ships with auras of colored light. Blue for USJ, red for Marianas, white around pieces of space junk or the larger remnants of ships caught by torpedoes.

The enemy destroyers are hammering at the *Inverness* and the escorts who protect her. Some smart pirate figured out that the drones had to be controlled from somewhere.

"Fire in the hold, fire in the hold."

Whoop, whoop. The *Inverness*'s Klaxon sounds. The most terrifying sound on the engineering deck, a wail of death.

"We're hit. Engineering to bridge, we're hit."

The screams of the burning and dying drown out the voice of the deck officer, but the message is clear.

"Status?"

"The bulkhead is sealed again, Chief."

"Engines overheating. Auto-shutdown is initiated. Shall I override?"

"Shit, no. Cool her off. No foam. No foam. It holds heat. No foam. Drag those hoses in here. Spray only, don't short any circuits."

The sound of crashing machinery followed by new screams brings the chief to the twisted, flaming control panel.

Two crewmen are pulling steaming junk off a pile, revealing a body that isn't moving.

"No, no, Smitty, no." An E5, his hands burned raw, cradles what is left of his comrade's head in his arms.

"Let her go, Riaz, let her go. She's gone." His buddy pulls him away from the body. Stunned, Riaz staggers mindlessly where he is shoved, grabs the hose nozzle, and drags it to the CT unit.

The spray hisses and spits, vaporizing against the hot metal and melting plastic. The chemical fog is more blinding than the smoke and not much kinder to the lungs.

The fire is brought under control. They finish the job with foam. Its engines shut down, the *Inverness* drifts through the battlefield, her guns still firing.

The Marianas command cruiser is so busy taking potshots at drones that it is too late when they see the destroyer jump forward, accelerating far beyond her safe limits. There would be broken bones and shattered piping throughout the ship. Before they can react the destroyer launches a well-aimed smart torpedo from near point-blank range.

The explosion cuts off the scream of fury from the pirate commander.

On board the destroyer her captain has the satisfaction of receiving a brief "well done" from Emerald. The acceleration has thrown them out of the range of the remaining pirates' guns and he allows himself a moment to relish the rare compliment.

By the time the destroyer reenters the battle zone, the enemy cruiser is a cloud of debris several kilos across. Still the few smaller ships remaining to the pirates fight back fanatically, knowing their fate if captured. Eventually the last is crushed by the sheer weight of fire from four destroyers.

"Ma'am," a staff lieutenant reports, still choking from the smoke on the bridge. "That was the last of them."

"Status," Emerald groans, also choking. She is still holding an empty fire extinguisher.

"Engine room is down. It's a shambles. Main engines seem to be okay, but they had a fire down there, and the auto cutoff engaged."

"Radio just went out," the communications tech reports. "We can't talk to anybody."

"Bad, very bad. What's the good news?" Emerald asks dismally.

She is told how many vessels survived, but their damage is not known and can't be assessed until communications are restored.

They have lost an hour on the battle, although it felt like it went on for days. Emerald paces the deck, tapping her stylus against her palm, waiting for an estimated time on repairs to her vessel and, eventually, her fleet.

Mark off 1 hour from your chart for the battle.

Roll one six-sided die. If the result is 4 or less, you have repaired the Inverness *in 1 hour. If it is greater than 4, you have not, and must continue rolling, losing 1 hour for each roll, until you roll a 4 or less. Subtract the lost hours from your time chart.*

Roll two six-sided dice. This is the number of drones that actually detonated in their attack on the pirates. Any remaining can be used, recovered, and used again.

Turn to section 62.

— **60** —

"Screw radio silence. Everybody and their pet dog in the sector already knows we're here. We might as well have sent out invitations. Beam it tight, in code. If anything gets through the space dust to the Marianas command, it isn't going to tell them much except that we have patrol ships. It's a risk, but it beats what's in second place.

"The main fleet can handle this wing if it's warned. No sweat. Our main fleet is their objective, so it's a percentage call whether they pursue or refuse attack against us. If they feel that we are the greater threat, they might just abandon their objective and hit us.

"If they figure they still have a chance to cause some

attrition on our task force, then they will disengage and steam on. In any case, our objective is clear. We need to hold them here and get across the Necklace ourselves to provide flanking fire against the enemy, even if they get wind that we are coming.''

She goes on as she outlines her plan to her subordinates. ''We can't use the drones, since the drone-jocks are running them from the command consoles aboard the *Inverness*, so deploy two destroyers and three escorts. That gives us slight inferiority to their cruiser-class ships, but it's close enough to even. Hit and run. Stay alive. But slow them up, or stop them. In any case, keep them off our backs.''

The ranking captain is already planning the tactics of his wing. He will use the principle of local superiority to even up the odds.

There are 5 ships in the squadron, to yield an Attack Strength of 35.

Since the navy is using very mobile tactics, and very sophisticated ones, they fire using Chart C.

The enemy, being less mobile, returns fire from Chart D.

If the navy destroys the enemy, turn to section 49.

If the enemy destroys the navy, turn to section 57.

— 61 —

Emerald's brow is wrinkled with concentration as she slowly outlines her thinking. ''Our main fleet is their objective, so it's a percentage call whether they pursue or refuse attack against us. If they feel that we are the greater threat, they just might abandon their objective and hit us.

''If they figure they still have a chance to cause some attrition on our task force, then they will disengage and steam on. In any case, our objective is clear. We need to get across the Necklace and provide flanking fire against the enemy, even if they get wind that we are coming.''

She goes on as she outlines her plan to her subordinates. "We can't use any drones, since the drone-jocks run them from the command consoles aboard the *Inverness*, so deploy two destroyers and three escorts. That gives us slight inferiority to their cruiser-class ships, but it's close enough to even. Hit and run. Stay alive. But slow them up or stop them. In any case, keep them off our backs."

The ranking captain is already planning the tactics of his wing. He will use the principle of local superiority to even up the odds.

There are 5 ships in the squadron, with an Attack Strength of 35.

Since the navy is using very mobile tactics, and very sophisticated ones, they fire using Chart C.

The enemy, being less mobile, returns fire from Chart D.

If the navy destroys the enemy, turn to section 49.

If the enemy destroys the navy, turn to section 58.

— 62 —

Emerald walks over to Dixon. "When is the last time you ate?"

"Oh, I guess—"

"Let's go eat." Emerald isn't really that hungry, but she can feel the tension depleting her resources. They hit the wardroom, where sandwiches, coffee, soft drinks, doughnuts and candy bars have been replenished throughout the flight.

"The ham and cheese is awful, but the only other choice is tuna fish, and it makes the bread too soggy for my taste."

Dixon grins and reaches for a tuna fish sandwich. "I rather like soggy bread," she says, and pours herself a coffee as well.

Emerald takes a pack of milk and a doughnut. Any more coffee and her stomach will go critical. They find a table and sit down.

"Holding up?" Emerald asks, watching Dixon unwrap the sandwich.

"Yes, ma'am, pretty well," Dixon replies.

"Only pretty well? This isn't your first action, is it?"

"No, ma'am. But, well, it's the first time I ever really took part, except to man my post. Command has a dark side, doesn't it?"

"Well, that makes it sound like evil sorcerers running around in capes," Emerald chortles, "but I know what you mean. Yes, you call the plays as best you can, and sometimes men and women die."

Dixon looks up at her, a slight frown clouding her dark eyes. "But I still love it—the thrill, the challenge. So am I so high on my adrenaline rush I'm forgetting the dark side?"

Emerald pauses before she replies. "I'm not the one to ask. You don't see me running off to farm an apple bubble or sell shoes. No, I really believe that we're doing something right, and we all asked to be in on it. Everyone in this command knows the risk. And whether you are a better person for putting on a show of agonizing over every loss . . . that's bull. We mourn our friends and comrades-in-arms, when we have the luxury to do so. In the meanwhile, we stay chill. The best memorial we can give the ones we lose, is to stay chill and finish the job."

"Thank you, ma'am."

They finish their food and return to the bridge after a detour to the head. They're both a lot more together after the break and the chance to share their fears.

Emerald's butt hasn't even warmed her chair when Lieutenant Phillips, the senior staff analyst from the *Sawfish*, spins around from his station and says, "There's a bogey ahead." He reels off the bearing and range.

"Okay. Let me know when you have visual."

Emerald is unconsciously breathing to the rhythm of the engine throb and the radar pings. The ship is almost an extension of her mind and will. She studies the glowing screen as the trace of the bogey drifts toward her flotilla.

"We've got it, ma'am. Oh, shit. Er, sorry—"

"Give me the good news, Phillips!" she responds, her voice steady but a trace of a smile on her lips.

"A Saturnian trawler, sir."

"Wonderful! I've got it," she said, now peering at her

own screen, the outline of the mining vessel distinct only to a trained eye.

The Union of Saturnine Republics deployed a large number of these vessels. They "dredged" fine dust and debris in gravity lens "nets," the resulting low-grade ore adding to the wealth and material independence of the state. They were the only major state to bother with the low-cost but low-yield operation since profit motive was not an issue.

Although ostensibly they were innocent enough, the real purpose of most of these mining ships was espionage. They certainly had the right to be in open space. Except for the fact that all Saturnian vessels were state owned, they fit into the category of civilian private enterprise. So they went where they willed and watched what they could.

Emerald knows that it would not be good form to blast the ship out of existence, as tempted as she is to do so. ("Oh, dear, Mr. Prosecuting Attorney, I am soooo sorry I shot down that little ol' mining boat. International incident? Oh, really?")

"What are they doing?" she inquires of the radioman.

"I can pick up a lot of telemetry activity. No long-range communication, though."

The trawler stabilizes her course out of practical firing range, far enough to indicate that she would just as soon avoid an incident, but close enough to take notes.

"Steady as she goes," Emerald croons, her attention never flagging as she scans the readouts. After two hours, close to the mouth of the Necklace, the trawler is still with them.

You have been cruising for 2 hours. Make note of this on your time chart.

If you have just run out of time, turn to section 29.

If you still have time, turn to section 73.

— **63** —

"What's the ordnance on that cruiser?" Emerald asks.

"We've got six eight-inchers, but the range is short. Probably rebuilt AJ-17s," the weapons tech replies.

The radar man calls out, "I've got a fix on Destroyer Number One. Two tubes, dumb bombs, but shielded."

"Command over there is a little flaky. The initial formation was good, but the response to the drone attack was weak. They overreacted," Phillips says.

"Good," Emerald says. "Pull in any remaining drones."

The task force has been warned, and the enemy firepower assessed and beamed to the *Sawfish*.

Emerald is tempted to finish them off but knows that her mission is more important. Any further risk of time or hardware is unacceptable.

"Disengage, and floor it," she snaps out.

As they swiftly move out of range, she wonders if the ranking pirate CO also is as dedicated to duty, or if he is going to cowboy and come after her.

Subtract ½ hour from your time sheet for the engagement.

Note the number of drones that remain.

Roll two six-sided dice.

If the number is the same as or less than your value for Stealth, turn to section 64.

If the number is greater than your value for Stealth, turn to section 65.

— **64** —

Emerald sits watching the radar screen as if she could move the ships on it by the force of her stare. Finally, she sees the remaining enemy fleet move away from her. She heaves a sigh of relief, pushing back the fleeting thought that she really should have nuked them. It was a stupid thought. The *Sawfish*, with her heavier armament, could engage them at dawn and still be in line for breakfast.

Turn to section 62.

— 65 —

Emerald sits watching the radar screen as if she could move the ships on it by the force of her stare.

"They aren't going away, ma'am."

"I can see that," she snaps at Lieutenant Phillips, the analyst who accompanied her from the *Sawfish*. Regretting that she lashed out, she adds, "Please calculate their speed and give me an ETA."

"Yes, ma'am," the young man replies, his shoulders relaxing slightly. He taps at his keyboard and pushes around tables with his stylus for a moment, then announces, "They are cruising at 2.9 gee. They're definitely falling behind us, but not very fast. That can't be their top speed, though. I'd figure 3.4 is a good guess."

"Thank you, Phillips. Well, now what?" she addresses her staff.

"I don't think they can catch up if we don't slow down," Dixon remarks.

"That's the rub. If we don't slow down. It's time again. Time has been the enemy this whole mission. By all rights we need to engage them and finish them. I don't like having a hyena pack on my tail. If we hit anything ahead, another Mayday, pirates, a Marianas scout, rocks, Santa Claus, anything, they'll be right up our ass. We're already critically behind schedule. Put your oars in, guys."

"I'd give them a sleigh ride. We can pilot the flotilla through every rough passage we hit. It's a risk to us, but we might lose them," Dixon suggests.

"Too radical. But how about this? We could give them a sleigh ride until we hit the first serious dust cloud. Then we bushwhack them," Phillips offers, grinning.

"Bushwhack?" the communications officer asks.

"Yeah, ambush them."

Emerald laughs at Phillips's obvious enthusiasm, made even more charming by his youth. The kid's over six foot six, has a shock of red hair that even a boot-camp shave wouldn't tame, and ears that stick out like jug handles. And a quick bugger with a stylus, to top it off.

"You almost have me convinced," Emerald admits. "But I just don't know about the extra risk. If we are going to hit them, why not just slow, wheel, and strike?"

Phillips looks somewhat abashed for having said something that someone might think was stupid.

"Whatever we do, I'd point out that their command didn't seem too stable in the last encounter, and we should have a free hand to control the fight," Dixon states. She brushes her short brown hair from her face.

"Thank you, officers." Emerald ends the conference, rising from the padded swivel chair at the command console. She knows she has a few minutes to make her decision and she needs a break.

She walks over to Dixon. "When is the last time you ate?"

"Oh, I guess—"

"Let's go eat." Emerald isn't really hungry, but she can feel the tension depleting her resources. They hit the wardroom, where sandwiches, coffee, soft drinks, doughnuts and candy bars have been replenished throughout the flight.

"The ham and cheese is awful, but the only other choice is tuna fish, and it makes the bread too soggy."

Dixon grins, and reaches for a tuna fish sandwich. "I rather like soggy bread," she says, and pours herself a coffee as well.

Emerald takes a pack of milk and a doughnut. Any more coffee and her stomach will go critical. They find a table and sit down.

"Holding up?" Emerald asks, watching Dixon unwrap the sandwich.

"Yes, ma'am, pretty well," Dixon replies.

"Only pretty well? This isn't your first action, is it?"

"No, ma'am. But, well, it's the first time I ever really took part, except to man my post. Command has a dark side, doesn't it?"

"Well, that makes it sound like evil sorcerers running around in capes," Emerald chortles, "but I know what you mean. Yes, you call the plays as best you can, and sometimes men and women die."

Dixon looks up at her, a slight frown clouding her dark eyes. "But I still love it, the thrill, the challenge. So am I so high on my adrenaline rush I'm forgetting the dark side?"

Emerald pauses before she replies. "I'm not the one to ask. You don't see me running off to farm an apple bubble or sell shoes. No, I really believe that we're doing something right, and we all asked to be in on it. Everyone in this command knows the risk. And whether you are a better person for putting on a show of agonizing over every loss . . . that's bull. We mourn our friends and comrades-in-arms, when we have the luxury to do so. In the meanwhile, we stay chill. The best memorial we can give the ones we lose, is to stay chill and finish the job.''

."Thank you, ma'am.''

They finish their food and return to the bridge after a detour to the head. They're both more together after the break and the chance to share their fears.

Emerald's butt hasn't even warmed her chair when Lieutenant Phillips spins around from his station and says, "Ma'am, the enemy has dropped off one vessel and is steaming toward us at 3.2. They're still not traveling at our speed, but they are keeping up.''

"Oh, great!'' Emerald exclaims.

If Emerald decides to keep on going, go to section 66.

If Emerald decides to turn and engage the pirates, go to section 67.

— 66 —

"Let's wait and see what they do. It's no loss for us; we're still making headway. Keep me posted.''

The bridge becomes quiet and patient, but tense, as they wait and watch.

"Ma'am, we have a bogey ahead.'' The radar tech reels off the bearing and range.

"Shit,'' Emerald hisses. She fights back the discouragement and guilt that threaten to flood her mind and screw up her judgment. *Okay girl*, she thinks, *you made the call, now make the play.*

"Ma'am?'' the helmsman inquires.

"What else is out there? Let me see.'' Blame and guilt are behind her now. The game is afoot, as some detective is reputed to have said. She can't remember the name and this bothers her precise mind; then Emerald is too distracted to stay annoyed.

"There, there is cover." She points to a group of unmoving blips and some streaks indicating a field of fine dust.

If Emerald decides to turn and fight, and she has drones left, turn to section 67.

If Emerald decides to turn and fight, and she has used all her drones, turn to section 69.

If Emerald decides not to engage, turn to section 68.

— 67 —

"I guess we haven't much choice," Emerald concludes. "Battle stations."

Again the Klaxon screams and men and women scramble. They have hardly stood down since the first bogey. And the mission is far from over.

Emerald is at her finest in this sort of battle. The chips are down, but she still gets to deal at least half the table.

"Captain, I want the *Inverness* to drop to a position in the rear of the fleet, but as far left as possible. This will give us some protection, but we can still pin the flank.

"Dixon, do you know the infantry tactic called 'Hammer and Anvil'?"

"Yes, ma'am. Pin one flank and roll the other. The *Inverness* is the anvil, correct?"

"Correct. String the big guns, destroyers and larger, along the right and then perform a wheel about to the right so that we present a line when the point of the enemy approaches firing range.

"Deploy lighter escorts with each larger ship. They have the speed to move to the front, unload, and drop back through the holes while the heavier ships give fire to cover them. We will fire in volleys, like the ancient infantry squares. First the escorts fire, then they drop back, then heavy fire and torpedoes from the heavy ships. If the enemy moves in, fire at will. If they retreat, we push them.

"What's left of the tugs? Send them to the right end of the line. They are the hammer. Each will launch its remaining drones, which will be on command control from the *Inverness*. Beef them up with a destroyer.

"Are the drone-jocks ready? Good. We crowd 'em. We roll 'em. Then we munch 'em."

The two fleets move into battle position, the ships' slow and ordered drift punctuated by sparkling staccato blasts of attitude rockets. It is like a stately ballet performed by steel whales.

You may use any remaining drones in this battle. They also may be used as losses from enemy fire. The enemy Attack Strength is figured by multiplying their number of ships times an Ordnance Value of 6.

The USJ navy fires using Chart C.

The pirates fire using Chart D.

Initial enemy strength:

Type	Ordnance
Cruiser	12*
Destroyer 1	6
Destroyer 2	6
Escort 1	6
Escort 2	6
Escort 3	6
Escort 4	6
Escort 5	6
Escort 6	6
Escort 7	6
Escort 8	6
Escort 9	6

If Emerald loses, or succeeds but has less than her required number of ships, turn to section 29.

If the navy destroys the enemy with enough ships to complete the mission, turn to section 71.

---

*Treat cruisers as 2 Ordnance 6 ships when calculating Attack Value, but 1 ship for losses.

— 68 —

"Let's get to some cover," Emerald decides. "We should be back behind the dust cloud by the time we pass the bogey. If it's harmless, we won't have slowed any. If not, we'll have evened our odds some."

Emerald is not thrilled with hiding, but she knows her objective and she has already made sacrifices to keep her fleet on course.

Soon they are thick in the cloud, the millions of tiny rock fragments sounding and feeling like sandpaper scraping endlessly on the hull.

"How much damage are we sustaining?" Emerald asks. "Keep me posted."

She feels suddenly very weary. They don't dare communicate with the other ships in the fleet, and Emerald is worried that this was a grave mistake. She wonders what this beating is doing to her birds.

"Bogey is still with us. I think she knows we're here. Either that or she is just real lucky!" Phillips says with grim humor.

"We're running out of cover, ma'am," Dixon announces, her lips pursed tightly with tension. "And the enemy is catching up."

"All right, let's use the time. Open a channel to the fleet. Let them know what's going on. Code. Now, let's round 'em up, and head 'em out," she finishes, winking at the very surprised Phillips, whose hobby is the Old West from Earth history.

"Damn it, Dixon," he whispers, "she doesn't miss anything, does she?"

"Nope," Dixon whispers back, suppressing a smirk.

Mark off ½ hour from your time chart for the delay in the "sand pit."

If Emerald has drones left, go to section 67.

If all her drones have been destroyed, turn to section 69.

— 69 —

"I guess we haven't much choice," Emerald concludes. "Battle stations."

Again the Klaxon screams and men and women scramble. They have hardly stood down since the first bogey, and it is far from over.

Emerald is at her finest in this sort of battle. The chips are down, but she still gets to deal at least half the table.

"Captain, I want the *Inverness* to drop to position in the rear of the fleet, but as far left as possible. This will give us some protection, but we can still pin the flank.

"Dixon, do you know the infantry tactic called 'Hammer and Anvil'?"

"Yes, ma'am. Pin one flank and roll the other. The *Inverness* is the anvil, correct?"

"Correct. String the big guns, destroyers and larger, along the right and then perform a wheel about to the right so that we present a line when the point of the enemy approaches firing range.

"Deploy lighter escorts with each larger ship. They have the speed to move to the front, unload, and drop back through the holes while the heavier ships give fire to cover them. If the enemy moves in, fire at will. If they retreat, we push them. What's left of the tugs? Send them to the right to support the escort. Together they are the hammer. Beef them up with a destroyer."

"Good. We crowd 'em. We roll 'em. Then we munch 'em."

The two fleets move into battle position, the ships' slow and ordered drift punctuated by sparkling staccato blasts of attitude rockets. It is like a stately ballet performed by steel whales.

The navy fires using Chart D.

The enemy fires using Chart D.

Initial enemy strength:

Type	Ordnance
Cruiser 1	12*
Destroyer 1	6
Destroyer 2	6
Escort 1	6
Escort 2	6
Escort 3	6
Escort 4	6
Escort 5	6
Escort 6	6
Escort 7	6
Escort 8	6
Escort 9	6

If Emerald loses, or prevails but has fewer than her required number of ships, turn to section 29.

If she destroys the enemy and has enough ships to complete the mission, turn to section 70.

*Treat as 2 Ordnance 6 ships when computing Attack Value and 1 ship for losses.

— 70 —

The enemy commander drops his flagship to the rear, concentrating the rest of his big guns to the van, their objective being the naval flagship. The navy seems to be stringing out the rest of its firepower fairly thinly, although he sees them begin to wheel so that they will engage his fleet in a line. He chuckles at the stupidity of the naval commander. All he has to do is realign his ships, rotating them around their own axes, and they will face the incoming naval line. And the naval rear is weak, depending on what looks to be a couple of tugs—fast tugs, but only tugs—and a couple of light escorts.

The steel-eyed pirate commander sits at a radar console much like the one aboard the *Inverness*. His military bearing makes his faded gray jumpsuit look as spit-and-polish as any navy admiral's.

"What the hell are they up to?" he mutters as he stares at his printout. "Gnats attacking elephants?"

But the surgical efficiency of the strike shocks him out of his assurance and complacency.

"Fire on them, damn it. Fire at will," the pirate commander bellows, the veins in his neck throbbing with fury.

But the first volley goes to the navy and the pirates suffer for it.

The pirate's destroyers begin hammering at the *Inverness* and the escorts who protect her. For a while the ships dance and fire in a silent, deadly light show of attitude jets and lasers. Then the *Inverness* hesitates for a second before skipping once more. There is no reason why, but the experienced gunners on the Marianas cruiser punch one through.

"Fire in the hold, fire in the hold."

Whoop, whoop. The *Inverness*'s Klaxon sounds, the most terrifying sound on the engineering deck, a wail of death.

"We're hit. Engineering to bridge. We're hit."

The screams of the burning and dying drown out the voice of the deck officer, but the message is clear.

"Status?"

"The bulkhead is holding, Chief."

"Engines overheating. Auto-shutdown is initiated. Shall I override?"

"Shit, no. Cool her off. No foam. No foam. It holds heat. No foam. Drag those water hoses in here."

The sound of crashing machinery followed by new screams leads the chief to the twisted, flaming control panel.

Two crewmen are pulling steaming junk off an unmoving body.

"No, no, Smitty, no." An E5, his hands burned raw, cradles what is left of his comrade's head in his arms.

"Let her go, Riaz, let her go. She's gone." His buddy pulls him away from the body. Stunned, Riaz staggers mindlessly where he is shoved, grabs the hose nozzle, and drags it to the CT unit.

The spray hisses and spits, vaporizing against the hot metal and melting plastic. The fog is more blinding than the smoke and not much kinder to the lungs.

The fire is brought under control moments before the water pressure fails. They finish the job with foam.

* * *

The Marianas command cruiser is so busy taking potshots at drones that they see the well-aimed smart torpedo coming at them from a naval destroyer too late.

The explosion cuts off the scream of fury from the pirate commander.

"Ma'am," a staff lieutenant reports, still choking from the smoke on the bridge. "That was the last of them."

"Status," Emerald groans, also choking. She is still holding an empty fire extinguisher.

"Engine room is down. It's a shambles. Main engines seem to be okay, but they had a fire down there, and the auto cutoff engaged."

"Radio is out," the communications tech reports. "We can't talk to anybody."

"Bad, very bad. What's the good news?" Emerald asks dismally.

She is told how many vessels survived, but their damage is not known and can't be assessed until communications are restored.

They have lost an hour on the battle, although it felt like it went on for days. And Emerald paces the deck, tapping her stylus against her palm, waiting for an estimated time on repairs to her vessel and her fleet.

Remove 1 hour from your chart for the battle. Remember, you have only 12 hours to complete your mission.

Roll one six-sided die. If the result is 4 or less, you have repaired the Inverness *in 1 hour. If it is greater than 4, you have not, and must continue rolling, losing 1 hour each time. Subtract the elapsed hours from your time chart.*

Turn to section 72.

— 71 —

The enemy commander drops his flagship to the rear, concentrating the rest of his big guns to the van, their objective being the naval flagship. The navy seems to be stringing out the rest of its firepower fairly thinly, although he sees them begin to wheel so that they will engage his fleet in a line. He chuckles at the stupidity of the naval commander. All he has to do is realign his ships, rotating them around their own axes, and they will face the incoming naval line. And the naval rear is weak, depending on what looks to be a trio of tugs—fast tugs, but only tugs.

Aboard the *Inverness*, Emerald is ready to release her secret weapon.

"Are the drones operational?"

"Yes, ma'am, and the drone-jocks plugged in."

"Let 'em rip."

The unassuming little tugs bloom and fizzle as their attitude rockets fire in tiny puffs, changing their courses and taking them to the front line.

Seated at a radar console, much like the one aboard the *Inverness*, is the steel-eyed pirate commander. His military bearing makes his faded gray jumpsuit look as spit-and-polish as any navy admiral's.

"What the hell are they up to?" he mutters, as he stares at his printout. "Gnats attacking elephants?"

His answer comes very soon. The tugs puff and glow once more, and then burst apart like opening flowers as the drones, which have been stowed like dead cargo on their hulls, glow into a life of their own and break away.

The tugs drop back, and now the enemy cruiser is facing nine very well armed wasps.

"Fire on them, damn it. Fire at will," the pirate commander bellows, the veins in his neck throbbing with fury.

But the first volley doesn't stop all the drones. Deep in the heart of the *Inverness*, drone pilots sit enclosed in egg-shaped command modules, oblivious to the ship around them, entranced by the immediacy of the battle taking place in the velvet, singing silence of space. Before each is a representation of space as seen by his drone, the three-dimensional screen ahead of them outlining ships with auras of colored light. Blue for USJ, red for Marianas, white around pieces of space junk or the larger remnants of ships caught by torpedoes.

The enemy destroyers are hammering at the *Inverness* and the escorts who protect her. Some smart pirate finally figured out that the drones had to be controlled from somewhere.

"Fire in the hold, fire in the hold."

Whoop, whoop. The *Inverness*'s Klaxon sounds, the most terrifying sound on the engineering deck, a wail of death.

"We're hit, Engineering to bridge. We're hit."

The screams of the burning and dying drown out the voice of the deck officer, but the message is clear.

"Status?"

"The bulkhead is holding, Chief."

"Engines overheating. Auto-shutdown is initiated. Shall I override?"

"Shit, no. Cool her off. No foam. No foam. It holds heat. No foam. Drag those water hoses in here."

The sound of crashing machinery followed by new screams leads the chief to the twisted, flaming control panel.

Two crewmen are pulling the steaming junk off an unmoving body.

"No, no, Smitty, no." An E5, his hands burned raw, cradles what is left of his comrade's head in his arms.

"Let her go, Riaz, let her go. She's gone." His buddy pulls him away from the body. Stunned, Riaz staggers mindlessly where he is shoved, grabs the hose nozzle, and drags it to the CT unit.

The spray hisses and spits, vaporizing against the hot metal and melting plastic. The fog is more blinding than the smoke and not much kinder to the lungs.

The fire is brought under control moments before the water pressure fails. They finish the job with foam.

The Marianas command cruiser is so busy taking potshots at drones that it is too late when they see the destroyer jump forward, accelerating far beyond her safe limits. There would be broken bones and shattered piping throughout the ship. Before they can react the destroyer launches a well-aimed smart torpedo from near point-blank range.

The explosion cuts off the scream of fury from the pirate commander.

On board the destroyer her captain has the satisfaction of receiving a brief "well done" from Emerald. The acceleration has thrown them out of the range of the remaining pirates' guns and he allows himself a moment to relish the rare compliment.

By the time the destroyer reenters the battle zone, the enemy cruiser is a cloud of debris several kilos across. Still the few smaller ships remaining to the pirates fight back fanatically, knowing their fate if captured. Eventually the last is crushed by the sheer weight of fire from four destroyers.

"Ma'am," a staff lieutenant reports, still choking from the smoke on the bridge. "That was the last of them."

"Status," Emerald groans, also choking. She is still holding an empty fire extinguisher.

"Engine room is down. It's a shambles. Main engines seem to be okay, but they had a fire down there, and the auto cutoff engaged."

"Radio is out," the communications tech reports. "We can't talk to anybody."

"Bad, very bad. What's the good news?" Emerald asks dismally.

She is told how many vessels survived, but their damage is unknown and can't be assessed until communications are restored.

They have lost an hour on the battle, although it felt like it went on for days. And Emerald paces the deck, tapping her stylus against her palm, waiting for an estimated time on repairs to her vessel and, eventually, her fleet.

Mark off 1 hour from your chart for the battle.

Roll one six-sided die. If the result is 4 or less, you have repaired the Inverness *in 1 hour. If it is greater than 4, you have not, and must continue rolling, losing 1 hour each time. Subtract the elapsed hours from your time chart.*

Roll two six-sided dice, again. This is the number of drones you used in the attack. Cross off these and any losses due to enemy fire from the Ship Loss Record Sheet.

Turn to section 72.

— 72 —

Emerald's butt hasn't even warmed her chair when Lieutenant Phillips spins around from his station and says, "There's a bogey ahead." He reels off the bearing and range.

"Let me know when you have visual."

Emerald is unconsciously breathing in the rhythm of the engine throb and the radar pings. The ship is almost an extension of her mind and will. She studies the glowing screen as the trace of the bogey drifts toward her flotilla.

"We've got it, ma'am. Oh, shit. Er, sorry—"

"Give me the good news, Phillips!" she responds, her voice steady but a trace of a smile on her lips.

"A Saturnian trawler, sir."

"Wonderful! Okay, I've got it," she says, now peering at her own screen, the outlines of the mining vessel distinct only to a trained eye.

The Union of Saturnine Republics deployed a large number of these vessels. They "dredged" fine dust and debris in gravity lens "nets." The resulting low-grade ore adds to the wealth and material independence of the state. They were the only major state to bother with the low-cost but low-yield operation, since profit motive is not an issue.

Although they appear innocent enough, the real purpose of most of these mining ships is espionage. They certainly had the right to be in open space. Except for the fact that all Saturnian vessels are state owned, they fit into the category of civilian private enterprise. So they went where they willed and watched what they could.

Emerald knows that it would not be good form to blast the ship out of existence, as tempted as she is to do. ("Oh, dear, Mr. Prosecuting Attorney, I am soooo sorry I shot down that little ol' mining boat. International incident? Oh, really?")

"What are they doing?" she inquires of the radioman.

"I can pick up a lot of telemetry activity. No long-range communication, though."

The trawler stabilizes her course out of practical firing range, far enough to indicate that she would just as soon avoid an incident but close enough to take notes.

"Steady as she goes," Emerald croons, her attention never flagging as she scans readouts. After two hours, close to the mouth of the Necklace, the trawler is still with them.

Mark off 2 hours from your time chart.

If you have just run out of time, turn to section 29.

If you still have time left, turn to section 73.

— 73 —

"Still out there?" Captain Hodges asks his communications officer, as he returns from the small refrigerator at the aft end of the bridge with a cold cola.

"Yes, sir. No change."

"Tell me, Brad, is this bogey making you as twitchy as it makes me?" Emerald asks him, leaning back in her chair, and trying to rub the pain out of her neck muscles.

"I don't know if I would feel safer with it gone. At least, now, we can keep an eye on it."

"You've got a point," she says, clicking her tongue, and pointing her finger like a pretend hand-laser at him.

But the tension is building, even though her people are pros, and in her book the best pros in the service.

"Okay," she says, heaving a sigh. Her staff and the whole bridge crew look up in response to the "okay," which is a sure sign that she is ready for action. "Let's rattle his cage. Open a channel, Sparks."

"This is the USJ *Inverness* to unknown vessel. Please identify yourself."

They wait impatiently for a response. Finally the crackle of an old, low-power transmitter is heard.

"This is the USR mining trawler *Kapusta*." Emerald notes that the E4 on duty on the bridge stifles a chuckle. The captain of the trawler is continuing, his hostility apparent even given the almost unintelligible communication link. "We are on a commercial civilian ore-gathering flight. Is this not international space?"

She cuts off her mike and asks the E4, a young man, "What is a *kapusta*?"

"A cabbage, ma'am," he answers.

She chuckles as she asks him, "You speak their lingo?"

"Yes, ma'am. I put in eighteen months at the Naval Language Training School."

"Good boy. Captain, may I have the use of this man for a while?"

"My pleasure," the captain answers. "Mendez?" The

man is relieved from his post and joins the command group at the large radar screen.

Emerald reopens the channel to the trawler. "This is Lieutenant Commander Emerald Sheller. We do not question your right to use these spaceways. We only wish to inquire as to your identity and to inform you that there has been serious pirate activity in this sector. We are patrolling for these criminals, as well as conducting a peaceful geological data survey, and are available to offer assistance if you have need, as a gesture of international friendship."

Out of sight of the video pickup, Dixon rolls her eyes and shakes her head. Phillips manfully suppresses a snicker.

The trawler captain's voice is still as chill as the backside of an asteroid. On the screen he visibly relaxes himself and assumes a cheerful smile that doesn't touch his eyes.

"We thank you for your concern, but we have had no problems with these pirates, and we hopefully will continue on our peaceful way."

"Would you agree to allow us to board you, solely for the purpose of offering you our expertise in defending yourself, should the occasion arise?"

"That is totally out of the question."

"As you wish. What is your current course? Perhaps you would find it advisable to move your operation away from our flotilla. You understand that I only have your safety in mind. We would be a likely target for a pirate raid, and an unarmed vessel such as yourself would do well to be clear of such an action."

"We are cruising toward our supply base, which is in the direct line of our current course. When we have reached our destination we will undoubtedly no longer find ourselves in the same section of this sector."

"Excuse me, Captain, but I didn't catch your name."

"That is because I did not give it. But if you wish to know, it is Mikhail Khukov. Now, if that is all you wished to know I shall end this communication. Out."

"You rather laid that on with a trowel, didn't you?" Captain Hodges says to Emerald, cocking his head to one side.

"That tub's captain look awfully academy for a miner," she muses.

"I noticed. If he isn't regular navy, or intelligence at the very least, I'll eat my hat."

"Dress or fatigue?"

"Either."

"It doesn't matter. You won't get a bet from me on that one. I'd give a month's pay for access to a naval intelligence data base." Emerald leans back over her chair and asks the linguist, "Spaceman, you were listening to the chatter. Did you pick up anything?"

"Only bridge talk. No, wait. Well, if it means anything—"

"Spit it out, man," the captain orders.

"The captain gave a command to improve the transmission, and the boatswain gave a response that is more common to the military than the merchant service. But a lot of merchant spacemen do a stint in the service, so that's pretty shaky intelligence."

"Nonetheless, it's a good observation. Well done," Emerald says, and adds to the captain, "I'd like this man to stay on the channel until we lose the buggers, with your permission."

The captain nods his approval and the man goes back to listening for Saturnian broadcasts.

They drift on toward the Necklace, still shadowed by the trawler.

"Ma'am, ma'am," the language expert shouts, "there's a message—" he begins.

But he is cut off by the radar controller. "There is a small object approaching the *Inverness*. Nonballistic velocity."

The communications officer cuts in, "We have it on visual. It appears to be a man in a pressure suit and jetpack approaching the ship."

"I've got it," Emerald snaps, scanning both her screen and the radar screen.

"There are a number of other blips, same size, several seconds behind him. He should be visible in a second."

Twang! The sound of gunfire hitting the hull jars the crew. It is only small-arms fire, but the integrity of the hull is something drilled into every child in a city bubble and reinforced time and again by combat experience.

"*Inverness* to *Kapusta*. Order your men to cease fire. *Now*!" Emerald commands, but she adds under her breath, "Or I'll roast your ass and claim they're a boarding party, you son of a bitch."

Now it is Captain Khukov's turn to snap an order. "There is a Saturnian citizen approaching your vessel. You will not interfere."

"The hell I won't, jerkoff," Emerald mutters, and says aloud, "Yes, and those are Saturnian citizens who are firing on a USJ naval vessel. Break off now, or I will return fire." Emerald barks over her shoulder to Captain Hodges, "Get that man on board."

The ting of another shot echoes loudly through the control room.

Hodges issues the order but looks back at her, his brow furrowed with concern.

"We don't have to keep him, Brad, but I'd just as soon get those goons with the firearms back on their own ship," she answers the unspoken protest.

"If you take that man on board, we shall attempt to board your vessel . . ." the radio crackles.

"The hell you will. Don't cut your career short, Lieutenant," Emerald shoots back, taking a calculated guess at the man's true rank in his nation's navy.

The other captain looks as if he is about to snap an order at Emerald, then catches himself once more. Judging from the curl of his lip, Emerald thinks to herself, she ranked him too low, and he resents it. *Okay, one for me*, she thinks wryly.

"Is that man on board yet?"

"Yes, ma'am."

"Good. Are his friends going home?"

"Yes, ma'am."

Dixon reports. "We've got Security down there, and Intelligence. We've got audiovisual tapes running."

"Good."

Dixon presses an ear-jack to her ear, and says, "They say the Saturnian just asked for political asylum."

Emerald squeezes her eyes closed and drops her head to her hand in sheer frustration. She quickly recovers and is out of her seat and headed off the bridge almost immediately.

"Dixon, you have the conn. I want to talk to this one myself. Spaceman, come with me." She gestures to the linguist, who trots after her.

Emerald jogs down the deck, her lithe, athletic body feeling tense and cramped from the long watch and the terrible responsibility. *Now what?* she wonders as she jumps the escalator to the lower decks, running the steps all the way. There is a very good chance that she has had the bum luck to acquire a real refugee, some member of a minority group or some lovesick puppy with a girl in the Jupe sector. Or she may have gotten a KGBS agent, with a sweet face and a great story.

As tough a lady as she is, she hates the thought of sending some misguided innocent back to his death, or worse. But she is on a military mission. This is no time to get involved in a thing like this. She needs more data. Maybe she can see through this guy, if he is no innocent.

"Officer on deck," the ranking noncom calls out.

"Where is he, the defector?"

"In the airlock, ma'am, but—" the spaceman starts.

But Emerald is already past him, and she already knows what he was going to say.

As the security team opens a path for her, she can see the defector just removing the helmet of the pressure suit.

The defector turns to face Emerald, her red hair in tight curls from sweat, and her big brown eyes staring hopefully.

The Saturnian stutters in broken English. "My name is Deena Abromovitz, and I beg political asylum."

"Oh, God," Emerald mutters. She struggles to control her confusion, and ambivalent feelings. Not one to practice a reverse sexism except to seek a fair shake for women who, like herself, have had to face discrimination, she still has a strong streak of sympathy and a stronger streak of the kind of chivalry that is encouraged in the service; that is, to protect the weak and oppressed even at great personal cost.

Before her stands a woman who is both threatened and a known oppressed minority in her homeland. Sheller is, for the first time in the mission, paralyzed. Struggling to regain her composure, she asks herself what she is going to do with this woman.

"Escort Ms. Abromovitz to the conference room on Deck 2B." Emerald manages to sound in control, playing for time. "I will be up presently. And bring us some coffee, please. You go, too." She gestures to the linguist, who is still in tow.

"Don't be afraid. Go with these people. They will take care of you," she assures the refugee, at the same time kicking herself for sounding so unneutral. Mendez translates and the woman smiles warmly at them both.

By the time Emerald has followed the security party up to the conference room, she has her composure back, helped by a splash of cold water in the face as she detours past her temporary quarters.

The Intelligence officer is already taking the defector's statement, mostly in English but sometimes through the interpreter.

"Lieutenant Ortez." Emerald beckons the Intelligence officer into the passageway. "Talk to me."

"It's the usual. Wants the good life, streets paved with gold, the whole thing. Plus some stuff on family problems. Discrimination, mostly. She claims, however, to have only a high school–level education, but she was on a mining trawler, and they don't let unskilled labor on trawlers. But, then again, they don't allow suspected security risks on trawlers either."

"Especially ones commanded by Captain Wonderful." ,

"What?"

"Nothing. Let me talk to her."

The woman tells her story again to Emerald, who once more feels a surge of sympathy for her. But this whole thing is taking time, and time is what they have little left of.

If Emerald chooses to let the woman stay, turn to section 74.

If Emerald chooses to send her back to the trawler, turn to section 75.

— 74 —

Damn it, Emerald chides herself, *I'm a USJ citizen and this woman wants to enjoy the freedom I take for granted.*

"I can't grant asylum, but I can give you permission to remain on board until you can get a fair hearing. You are now on USJ property and under my protection."

Emerald turns on her heel and leaves before the woman can unnerve her even more with her oversized eyes.

"Lieutenant," she barks at the Intelligence officer as she breezes past him. He follows her out into the passageway, shutting the soundproof door behind him. "It still makes me twitchy to have her on board. I want her locked up and watched. But I also want her interrogated. If she's so anxious to join our side she might be able to tell us what her former comrades are up to out there."

"Yes, ma'am, I'll work with her. The only secure holding facility is the brig, which isn't really conducive to making folks feel at home."

"That's okay. If she's for real she'll be expecting a little hassle, and if she's not she'll, well . . . she'll be expecting a little hassle," Emerald finishes with a guffaw.

The Intelligence officer chuckles and suggests humorously, "Maybe we can pretty up her cell."

"Well, some coffee might be a good start. I understand the other side is short of the stuff, but navy chow might be counterproductive. Nobody eats as badly as we do!"

"Yes, ma'am. I'll take care of her."

"Regular reports."

"Yes, ma'am."

The lieutenant rejoins the new passenger while Emerald returns to her post on the bridge.

"Dixon, how is our civilian escort doing?" she asks, slipping into her chair.

"The trawler captain has been screaming up a storm. We have him on line, if you want to talk to him."

"Wouldn't miss it for the world. Put him on."

"Commander, I must object—" he begins, without preamble or amenities as soon as his face appears on her screen.

"I'm sure you must. Your former crew member is safely aboard, and will remain so until we complete our scientific survey and return to port. At which time she will be turned over to the proper authorities. Your government is certainly within its rights to protest this action, as I expect you shall. However, for the safety of a civilian, and for the safety of my ship, I have taken this action. Again I warn you that there has been pirate activity, and although we are on a peaceful mission we certainly will fire on any pirates we encounter. Or fire back when fired upon. It would be better if you returned to your own base."

The trawler captain only grunts before cutting off transmission, but his ship shadows the flotilla for some time before it eventually heads off toward a medium-sized planetoid.

"Ma'am, I just picked up a transmission. Could we get our translator back?"

"Do it," Emerald orders, and the young crewman is recalled to the bridge.

He listens to a replay of the communications pickup, tapping notes on his console, and then reports. "The trawler is sending a report on the defection. Let's see . . . he identified us. Class, tonnage, armament of every ship we have,'' he mutters as he finishes scribbling. Then he reads back the entire transmission.

Emerald no longer has a doubt that this mining vessel is a full-bore spy ship. But what really worries her is that the whole universe has just been treated to a detailed description of her flotilla.

"So much for secrecy. Let's make tracks, people. Speed's all we've got left. Thank you, Mendez,'' she says to the linguist. "Stay with Intelligence for a while.'' she orders, dismissing him.

"Phillips, what's our ETA to the Necklace?''

"We should reach the mouth in about thirty-five minutes.''

"Deploy a couple of birds. I want a good look.''

The patrol is ordered to fly, and Emerald settles into the "hurry up and wait'' attitude that marks much of a military career. About twenty minutes have passed when the radioman leans forward at his station, his hand pressing his ear-jack firmly into his ear. Emerald snaps to attention as he turns to report. The look on his face is grim and serious.

"Ma'am, there is a transmission to the Saturnian base. It's coming from the *Inverness*.''

"Captain,'' she says sharply, "we have a problem.''

The *Inverness* is her flagship, but it is Brad's command.

The captain of the *Inverness* briskly orders the radioman, "Sparks, let's see where that signal is coming from.''

With the economy of movement that marks a professional, the radioman initiates a search to find the origin of the transmission, the familiar plans of the vessel displayed on the console screen. In moments, a yellow blinking spot is isolated in a companionway leading to the main engine room.

Emerald feels a stab of guilt. The defector. Of course. And she is responsible for letting the woman stay.

Captain Hodges orders security forces to surround the area, and he sends a warning to the engine room that there is a Saturnian agent heading their way.

Emerald heads off the bridge at a dead run. She is responsible and she is going to deal with the problem.

She arrives at the hatch to the companionway behind a squad of armed security guards.

"Stay back, ma'am,'' the sergeant says firmly as he gestures with his rifle for his point man to move through the opening and down the stairs.

Emerald draws her side arm and drops back behind the sergeant. She can see Abromovitz and the translator, Mendez, huddled at the turn of the steel stairway.

"Move down and take her out," the sergeant orders his squad, who scurry to what little cover the open grillwork of the staircase offers, working their way down for a clear shot. One of the men levels his sights on his target.

Without thinking, Emerald shouts, "*No!*"

Roll two six-sided dice.

If the number rolled is less than or equal to the fleet's value for Morale, turn to section 76.

If the number is greater than the value for Morale, turn to section 77.

— 75 —

Emerald eyes the woman. It is all too pat. Despite her wonderfully sad, oversized eyes, the woman has the carriage and deportment of something other than a low-ranking crew member aboard a second-rate mining trawler. In OCS they called it command presence.

Suddenly, the weight of pity and sympathy Emerald has been carrying snaps away. *Shit, girl,* she thinks to herself, *this is like you trying to pass yourself off as some fresh-off-the-farm mammy. This is bullshit. You're an officer in the USJ Navy and this woman is an officer in the USR something or other. That's as plain as the nose on your face. Don't be a chump. Get rid of her.*

Behind the rationalization the fear persists that if she is wrong, she is condemning this woman to death, or worse, at the hands of a government she believes to be despotic and totalitarian. But the realization that she is not on a peaceful cruise but on a war mission clears her head. She has no right to take a foreign national, and a civilian at that, into a battle zone.

"I'm sorry, Ms. Abromovitz. I will have to return you to your ship. I'm sure we can convince your captain that you suffer from an excess of romanticism and with any luck you will be able to talk your way out of a serious criminal charge. No, don't start crying. This is the way it is and it can't be helped." Mendez moves to console the woman and holds her as she shakes. He gives his commander a scathing look and then looks away. Emerald turns her back on the sobbing woman and returns to the bridge.

"Dixon, how is our civilian escort doing?" she asks, slipping into her chair.

"The trawler captain has been screaming up a storm. We have him on-line, if you want to talk to him."

"Wouldn't miss it for the world. Put him on."

"Commander, I must object—" he begins, without preamble or amenities as soon as his face appears on her screen.

"I'm sure you must. Your crew member is safely aboard. I feel that the woman was a little carried away with a romantic notion. When I talked to her, we agreed that she should return to your vessel. Although we are on a scientific survey, we are apt to run into pirates, and we are authorized to return fire. This is no place for a civilian." The emphasis that Emerald puts on the last word makes her crewmates wince, but the Saturnian captain does not react. Emerald decides she does not wish to play poker with him at any time now or in the future.

She continues, "We shall send a shuttle with a squad of armed guards. We will dock with your vessel according to international regulations. We will not board your vessel, and you will not board our shuttle except to send two unarmed persons to escort your crew member into your ship. After the transfer, I suggest that it would be better if you returned to your own base."

As agreed upon, the transfer is made. Emerald does not leave the bridge during the transfer, and she tries hard not to question her own judgment in this matter.

The trawler again shadows the flotilla for some time before it eventually breaks off, heading toward a medium-sized planetoid.

"Ma'am, I just picked up a transmission. Could we get our translator back?"

"Do it," Emerald orders, and the young crewman is recalled to the bridge.

He listens to a replay of the communications pickup, tapping notes on his console, and then reports, "The trawler is sending a report on the defection. Let's see . . . he's identified us. Class, tonnage, armament of every ship we have, and in the clear," he mutters as he finishes scribbling. Then he reads back the entire transmission. Emerald no longer has any doubts in the world that this mining vessel is a full-bore spy ship. But what really worries her is that the whole universe has just been treated to a detailed description of her flotilla.

"So much for secrecy. Let's make tracks, people. Speed's all we've got left. Thank you, Mendez," she says to the linguist.

"Ma'am, may I leave the bridge for a few minutes? That was a workout. I haven't spoken Saturnian for a couple of years, and, well, I could use a cup of coffee before I resume my watch."

"Yeah, sure. That episode was rough on all of us. Take fifteen minutes and then report back to the captain."

"Thank you, ma'am," he says, and leaves the bridge.

"Phillips, what's our ETA to the Necklace?"

"We should reach the mouth in about thirty-five minutes."

"Deploy a couple of birds. I want a good look."

The patrol is ordered to fly, and Emerald settles into the "hurry up and wait" attitude that marks much of a military career. About twenty minutes have passed when the radioman leans forward at his station, his hands pressing his ear-jack firmly into his ear. Emerald snaps to attention as he turns to report. The look on his face is grim and serious.

"Ma'am, there is a transmission to the Saturnian base. Its origin is the *Inverness*."

"Captain," she says sharply, "we have a problem."

The *Inverness* is her flagship, but it is Brad's command.

Captain Hodges briskly orders the radioman, "Sparks, let's see where that signal is coming from."

With the economy of movement that marks a professional, the radioman initiates a search to find the origin of the transmission, the familiar plans of the vessel displayed on his console screen. In moments, a yellow blinking spot is isolated in a companionway leading to the main engine room.

"Sparks, can you make out the content of the transmission?"

"No, sir, it's some sort of code. It's being beamed toward that Saturnian base asteroid."

Captain Hodges orders security forces to surround the area,

and he sends a warning to the engine room that there is a Saturnian agent heading their way.

"Where the hell is that translator? Where is Mendez?" Emerald shouts. Suddenly she feels a sick sinking feeling in her gut. Mendez. Could he be in cahoots with the woman? Could this have been a setup to give the trawler close access to the naval vessel? But how would they know we were here? It was a secret mission. A target of opportunity? A much higher-level leak than Emerald wants to even think about? In that sticky slow motion that marks emergencies and crises, Emerald's mind is a jumble of conflicting thoughts. But one thing is certain: she has a spy on board, and Mendez is suspect number one.

She leaves the bridge at a dead run. She wants to see this firsthand. She arrives at the hatch to the companionway behind a squad of armed security guards.

"Stay back, ma'am," the sergeant says firmly as he gestures with his rifle for his point man to move through the opening and down the stairs.

Emerald draws her side arm and drops back behind the sergeant. She can see the translator, Mendez, huddled at the turn of the steel stairway.

"Move down and take him out," the sergeant orders his squad, who scurry to what little cover the open grillwork of the staircase offers, working their way down for a clear shot. One of the men levels his sights on his target.

"No," Emerald bellows, "I want him alive. Okay, bastard, your ass is mine."

"Hold your fire!" the sergeant bellows.

Emerald is past him and sprinting down the stairs, ignoring the little voice in her head telling her that grandstanding is out of bounds for a commanding officer. She sees a glint of a weapon and throws herself down the stairs in a shoulder roll and springs straight into the huddled man. There is a flash of laser fire. She can smell the sweet odor of burning hair as it flushes past her face. One eye is filled in colored sparks from the aftereffect of the near-miss. Emerald grabs her assailant's wrist and twists Mendez's arm back and up, punching to the back of his arm just above the elbow. Emerald enjoys the satisfying crunch as she hears it snap.

He screams in pain and she throws a palm into his face, striking his jaw as he turns away from the blow. Still in a frenzy of motion, Emerald chops to the back of his neck,

pulling the blow as it lands so that Mendez crumples unconscious, but not dead, at her feet. For a moment no one moves
except Emerald, still panting gestures for a security man to
revive the translator.

Mendez groans and holds his head as he comes to. She
grabs the man by his good arm and muscles him roughly up
the stairs. In the corridor, she slams him against the bulkhead, spins him around, and in her most efficient military-
police fashion, frisks him. She quickly finds the transmitter.
It is small enough to have been passed to him during that
touching scene with the "defector."

"Why?" she can barely ask through her fury.

"Why?" he repeats. "Why? Maybe this chicken-shit outfit
is enough for you. Do you think anything is going to change
because you and your precious Captain Hubris managed to
get a few bars and stripes for guys named Juan or Rastez?
The lily-white majority will never give up their power peace-
fully. Why don't you join me and we can take it together?"
The translator looks at Emerald expectantly. It takes her a few
seconds to realize he is really looking for an answer. She
turns red with fury and gestures for the security patrol to grab
him.

"¡Viva la revolucion!" Mendez cries, but already there is a
tremor in his voice. He winces at the pain from his arm.

"Take him away," Emerald says with terrifying control.
As the armed guards surround him she adds, "Maybe you'll
get a chance to try out the other side . . . if we don't execute
you when we get home. By the way, what did you transmit?"
she asks, not really expecting an answer.

"The plans for the new antitorpedo tracking system," he
gloats, as the guards drag him off. "Admiral Ivanov was
quite anxious for them. I don't think he liked you, though."
His grin turns to a grimace as a spaceman twists his broken
arm.

Emerald returns to the bridge, settles into her chair, and
sends an aide for a cup of coffee, ignoring the acid in her
stomach.

"Have we heard from the birds, yet?"

"So far, so good," Captain Hodges replies.

"Good," she says, rubbing her eyes. "Keep me posted."

"Badger, do you copy? I say there is a clear passage,
except for some golf balls. We are going in. Follow me."

"I hear you, Surfer. Did you bring your clubs?"

But before he can end his transmission, Badger sees through his aft port the brilliant burst that was his friend.

"Mother Hen, Mother Hen. We've hit a mine field. Do you copy?" he screams into the mike, as he desperately tries to alter his course. He drifts too close to a proximity fuse and joins his buddy as a name on some war memorial.

Cross 2 "chicks" off the Ship Loss Record Sheet. If none are left, then escorts or destroyers must be lost. Then continue reading.

When the word is relayed to the bridge, Emerald is stunned. The Necklace had been clear the last time she sent recon. Now she has lost two more ships and good men.

"Dixon, let's see the maps." Dixon brings up a computer image of the latest and most detailed charts of the area. Unfortunately, they are not detailed enough. The command staff and the captain study them, rotating and shifting magnification, looking for another route. Nothing is showing up.

"How long would it take the minesweeper *Risk* to clear the area?"

"Even if she shotgunned shrapnel to detonate the passage, it would take a couple of hours. For her to locate and neutralize the passage, probably about four hours."

"Oh, great. Keep looking," Emerald says, with forced calm.

"Wait. I've got something. There." Phillips focuses in on the faint track of black, indicating a break in the hull-tearing sand trap.

"Well, do we go for it?" Emerald asks, staring at her staff. "Let's not all answer at once," she adds wryly, when no one offers an opinion.

"It could be safe, or it could be a cul-de-sac. If it is, we'd never be able to backtrack in time to clear the mines and make our objective. It's an unknown," Dixon says, her face drawn with strain.

"I agree," the captain offers.

"Unfortunately, so do I," Emerald says. "Let's get the *Risk* out there."

Boom! Boom! Boom! Boom!

The *Risk* sweeps back and forth across the mouth of the

passage, finding and detonating the hundreds of mansized mines that are virtually undetectable from the thousands of pieces of debris littering even this "clear" area in the asteroid belt.

Each explosion, silent in the vacuum of space, jars and rattles the *Inverness* and her escort with jaw-clenching vibration as shock and shrapnel pelt against the fragile hull.

"Damn it, when will it be done?" Emerald mutters quietly. Her impatience is shared by every officer and crewman on the bridge. She is wearing her shoulders up around her ears with tension, waiting for the next blast, when she realizes she hears only wonderful silence.

"We have a transmission from the *Risk*."

"*Risk* to *Inverness*. The area is clear. We repeat, the area is clear."

"Thank God," Emerald sighs. "Move 'em out."

You are lucky. The Risk *does the job in about 1 hour. Remove 1½ hours from your time sheet for cruising time and for the minesweeper to clear the passage.*

If you have run out of time, turn to section 29.

If you have time, turn to section 78.

— 76 —

"Hold your fire!" As the sergeant bellows, Emerald is past him. She sees the glint of a weapon, and she throws herself down in a shoulder roll, and slams straight into the huddled couple. There is a flash of laser fire. She can smell the sickly-sweet odor of burning hair as the beam scorches past her. For a brief instant the commander is blinded by the afterglow of the near-miss. Sheller grabs the wrist of her assailant, and twists Mendez's arm back and up, punching hard to the back of his elbow. She enjoys the satisfying crunch as she hears it snap.

Mendez screams in pain, and Emerald throws a palm strike to his face. It snaps against his jaw as the beleaguered translator turns away from the blow. His head snaps back and bounces off the corridor wall. He recoils to stumble dazed in front of the USJ officer.

Still in a frenzy of motion, Emerald chops to the back of his neck, pulling the blow as it lands, so that Mendez crumples unconscious, but not dead, at her feet.

"Oh, thank you. He forced me," the defector starts to babble, crying copiously.

"Save it, lady. Sergeant, would you clean up here? And you," she shouts savagely at Abromovitz, "you are coming with me!"

She grabs the woman by the arm and muscles her roughly up the stairs. In the corridor, she slams the woman against the bulkhead, spins her around and, in her most efficient military-police fashion, frisks her. She quickly finds the transmitter. It's a small device, barely a few inches wide and less than an inch thick. Trailing wires showed how it used the ship's hull as an antenna. Still, it was unlikely to have broadcast farther than the "trawler." Though Emerald is sure this was far enough for the traitor's protests.

"He put it there," the woman protests.

"Yeah, sure." Emerald knows that she may be wrong, and that the woman may be telling the truth, but there was something in the way that Mendez and Abromovitz were huddled that didn't ring true if he was holding her hostage, or if she was holding him hostage, either.

How the defector got loose could be discovered when there was time for an investigation, but clearly this was a setup of some sort.

"Lock her in the forward security cabin," Emerald orders, still panting.

As she is dragged away, Abromovitz calls out in apparent panic. "Please, I'll confess. Only please, listen to me. We are steering for a minefield." The woman's face is white with fear. She struggles to turn and face the other woman.

"What! Wait, bring her back," Sheller snaps. The security guards drag her, not too kindly, back to where Emerald is standing.

The "defector" blurts out her plea as if fearing she will not be allowed to finish. Her eyes beg for trust from the tall black woman in front of her. "Listen to me. It is true. I am an officer in the KGBS. I was supposed to attempt to infiltrate your country. I did not know about Mendez, although my superiors might have. He had taken plans for the new antitorpedo tracking system and was looking for an opportunity to send them to our side. When I boarded he decided to use me as a cover to send the message and if caught, to blame me. He would have killed me before I could be interrogated. He knew I would have a communicator to inform Admiral Ivanov, your 'lieutenant,' of my success. I don't know if my own side betrayed me, or if I was just some target of opportunity for Mendez. Maybe Ivanov sent me over for him to use. In doesn't matter anymore, I have no wish to die. You are heading directly for a minefield. I can navigate you through it, if you are willing to trust me."

The spy stops talking abruptly, her eyes locked on the USJ officer's face a few feet away.

"Bring her to the bridge," Emerald orders the guards as she coldly stares at the woman. The helpless look is gone from the woman's eyes, replaced by a mixture of smoldering anger and genuine fear.

"Oh, shit," Emerald mutters, "the birds." She trots to the nearest intercom box and slams down the code button. "Sheller to bridge. Recall the recon birds. *Now!*"

"Badger, do you copy? I say there is a clear passage, except for some golf balls. We are going in. Follow me."

"I hear you, Surfer. Did you bring your clubs?"

"Mother Hen to Chicks. Break off, break off."

"What the hell! Well, if they say so, we're going home."

The two recon vessels change course to return to the flotilla, unaware that they are within meters of setting off the proximity fuses on the string of mines.

On the bridge of the *Inverness*, good to her word, the Saturnian officer points out the area of the minefield. It is strung directly across the mouth of the Necklace.

"Is there a way around this?"

"Yes," Major Abromovitz answers. She points out an almost invisible passage just starboard of the minefield. "You will lose a little time, but it beats the alternative."

Emerald watches the woman as she settles into the easy air of command. The commander wanders off and brings back two cups of coffee.

"Thanks," the Saturnian says, accepting the cup.

Emerald nods back, then asks, "Tell me, though. I just don't understand. Why?"

"Why what?"

"Why someone like you is KGBS. I mean, you are a Saturnian minority, and—"

"Oh, that. It shouldn't be so hard for you to understand. You are black. Do you run around in a head scarf and eat chitlins and pones, and pick cotton? No, you are an officer in your country's navy. I think we are much alike. I believe in my country, too. I am not enslaved by any cultural, racial, or religious background. My family have been ranking officers and party members for generations. I was given an assignment. My only regret is that I failed. I will undoubtedly be traded back to my own planet, and I will have to answer for my failure, although I must admit that I would like some answers about Mendez's presence on this ship. But, that is another problem for another day. Today we must avoid mines."

They maneuver into the small but clear passage, and into the Necklace, at last.

Mark off a total of ½ hour from your time sheet.

Turn to section 78.

— 77 —

The crewman holds the Saturnian woman in his sights. He hears the officer shouting and thinks, *What is that crazy bitch shouting about?* He hears the sergeant shout, "Hold your fire." *Like Hell. Hold fire? For a commie? Hell, no!* He fires. Deena Abromovitz crumples to the deck, a jagged valley of burnt flesh cut into her back and shoulder.

The sergeant turns with an expression on his face that makes the crewman back into the bulkhead. "Briggs, I said hold your fire."

"You did, Sarge? It all happened so fast."

There will be an investigation, but they both know it will come to nothing. Briggs acted under orders. Under the tension of a shoot-out, it was perfectly believable that he didn't hear the original order countermanded. At least, that's what they would all say. There is little sympathy for a spy, less maybe for a dead one.

Emerald rushes down the iron grillwork staircase, her footsteps echoing hollowly in the companionway. The woman is dead. With a look of disgust, Emerald runs her hands over the body and finds the transmitter.

"Oh, thank God," Mendez mutters. A small laser pistol lies on the deck at his feet. He appears shaken and sags against a nearby hatch.

"How did this happen?" Sheller demands.

"Lieutenant Green stepped out, and Abromovitz overpowered the guard, took his weapon, and held me at gunpoint. She was heading for the engine room. She stopped to send a message in code. I don't know what she was going to do next. Maybe blow the ship."

Something is still missing, a voice in Emerald's head insists, as she listens to this heartfelt outpouring from the rescued crewman. Something is not right. But she holds her peace and orders the crewman to his quarters pending an investigation.

"Sergeant, clean up this mess." she orders brusquely, and returns to the bridge.

Once there, she settles into her chair, and sends an aide for a cup of coffee.

"Have we heard from the birds, yet?" Emerald asks the communications tech.

"So far, so good."

"Good," she says, rubbing her eyes, "keep me posted."

"Badger, do you copy? I say there is a clear passage, except for some golf balls. We are going in. Follow me."

"I hear you, Surfer. Did you bring your clubs?"

But before he can end his transmission, Badger sees through his aft port the brilliant burst that was once his friend.

"Mother Hen, Mother Hen. We've hit a minefield. Do you copy?" he screams into the mike, as he desperately tries to alter his course. He drifts too close to a proximity fuse, and joins his buddy as a name on some war memorial.

Cross 2 birds off the Ship Loss Record Sheet. If there are no birds left, eliminate the escorts or destroyers you launched in their place. If this means you have less than 5 ships left, turn to section 29. If you have more than 5 ships left, continue reading.

When the word is relayed to the bridge, Emerald is stunned. The Necklace had been clear the last time she sent recon. She has lost two more ships, and good men.

"Dixon, let's see the maps." Dixon brings up a computer image of the latest and most detailed charts of the area. Unfortunately, they are not detailed or late enough. The command staff and the captain study them, rotating and shifting the magnification, looking for another route. Nothing is showing up.

"How long would it take the minesweeper *Risk* to clear the area?"

"Even if she shotgunned shrapnel to detonate the passage, it would take a couple of hours. For her to locate and neutralize the passage, probably about four hours."

"Great. Keep looking," Emerald says with forced calm.

"Wait. I've got something. There." Phillips focuses in on the faint track of black, indicating a break in the hull-tearing sand trap.

"Well, do we go for it?" Emerald asks, staring at her staff. "Let's not all answer at once," she adds wryly, when no one offers an opinion.

"It could be safe, or it could be a cul-de-sac. If it is, we'd never be able to backtrack in time to clear the Necklace mines and make our objective. It's an unknown," Dixon says, her face drawn with strain.

"I agree," the captain offers.

"Unfortunately, so do I," says Emerald. "Let's get the *Risk* out there."

Boom! Boom! Boom! Boom!

The *Risk* sweeps back and forth across the mouth of the passage, finding and detonating the hundreds of midsized mines that are virtually undetectable from the thousands of pieces of debris littering even this "clear" area in the asteroid belt.

Each explosion, silent in the vacuum of space, jars and rattles the *Inverness* and her escort with jaw-clenching vibration, as shock and shrapnel pelt against the fragile hull.

"Damn it, when will it be done?" Emerald mutters quietly. Her impatience is shared by every officer and crewman on the bridge. She is wearing her shoulders up around her ears with tension, waiting for the next blast, when she realizes she hears only wonderful silence.

"We have a transmission from the *Risk*."

"*Risk* to *Inverness*. The area is clear. We repeat, the area is clear."

"Thank God. Move 'em out."

The Risk *does the job in about 1 hour. Mark off 1½ hours from your time sheet for cruising time and for minesweeper to clear the passage.*

If you have run out of time, turn to section 29.

If you have time left, turn to section 78.

— 78 —

The flotilla tightens up her cruising order, which resembles a long porcupine with the flagship in the middle and extra firepower at the van and rear. But battle losses have thinned the skin of this steel monster. Emerald finds herself glancing at the time readout more and more often.

But they are in the Necklace, at last. And that perks up her morale. They're in the home stretch.

"Commander Sheller, we have company," Phillips reports crisply, not letting his exhaustion show in his eyes or in his voice.

Emerald forces back the groan she feels and squares her shoulders as she looks over at the big radar screen. All she sees is background crud, but she knows that she isn't really very focused anymore. The endless cups of coffee have given her a buzz she can feel down to her toes, and the repeated jolts of adrenalin as crisis after crisis has had to be faced and fought have left her aching in every joint and muscle.

"Once more into the breach, dear friends," she says wearily, drawing a certain kind of resigned power from the quote. *Yeah, Shakespeare hit it on the head in that play. King Henry knew the bittersweet responsibility of command.* She fights to remember the whole quote but can only keep hearing the phrase "or stop up the . . . the something or other . . . with our English dead." She decides she would make an unlikely Englishman at best and smiles at the thought.

Sheller sets to decoding the blips and smudges on the screen. Her eyes refuse to focus at first, the screen blurring in and out of sight. Then the surge of battle rushes through her tired frame and everything is in painfully sharp focus.

"Phillips, show me," she orders briskly.

"Watch here, and here. Just keep watching. There, did you see that?"

"Yeah, I think so. Couldn't just be an erratic orbit or some anomaly caused by the gravity lenses? Sometimes we broadcast a shadow, and things move funny."

"Don't think so, ma'am. I've been watching it . . . two more points and I can plot . . . there, and there. Got it."

He buries himself in his terminal for a few minutes and then a scroll of information and charts rolls up onto his screen.

"They are under power, and there are more than one of them. In fact there seem to be . . . oh, my God!"

The band of space debris and asteroids that the task force had dubbed the Sajo River was tactically useful because it slowed up traffic and provided cover for ambush. This second point was the rationale behind Emerald's whole expedition. But it was also ideal cover for anybody else who knew about it. You not only could hide a fleet in it, but someone had. The task force is rushing into the center of dozens of unmoving ships. Trapped by the debris in every direction, there is no way they can turn aside.

"So much for our secret passage. It looks like we're surrounded, doesn't it?" She sighs, regaining the steely-eyed combat readiness she is trained for and will need to get her flotilla out of this alive. "Who are we facing? Any guesses? If it's Saturnians we should be able to talk our way out. The guess at high command these days is that they aren't hot for Solar War III. If it's some crazy Arabs off Mars, it's anybody's guess. They'll be off on an interplanetary jihad of their own, but they aren't too careful about who they shoot at. It must be nice to believe you've got Allah on your side."

"I'm getting some configurations," Phillips reports. "It's a scrap heap of a fleet, but it's big. Pirates, I'd guess. Some of those read like merchant ships with a few turrets rigged."

"Oh, bloody hell," the captain groans, slapping his forehead.

"What is it, Brad?" Emerald asks.

"There's been a rumor going around about a hiding place, sort of a bandit hideout, renegade captains and the like. I think we just found it. If they were Marianas, they'd be with the fleet facing Hubris.''

''Any chance we can just sneak past?'' Emerald asks hopefully. ''Will they seek us out and engage us? They have to know we are here.''

''Beats me. It's worth a try. I mean, if we don't bother them, they might not bother us. We can try to hold to the lower side of the passage, away from the bulk of them. Maybe not look too unfriendly,'' Brad suggests.

Emerald wonders how several warships sailing through the center of a secret pirate rendezvous could look anything but unfriendly. She keeps her doubts quiet and the navigator continues.

''These aren't soldiers, they're pirates. My brother is a cop in the Chitown bubble. It's not uncommon for street gangs to avoid confrontation. I think there is some analogy here. They have nothing to gain starting something with us. On the other hand, if they're crazy enough, they might try to hit us for supplies, to say nothing of the macho value of beating the USJ Navy.''

''Okay,'' she says, moving into action, ''send a communiqué to all ships. 'Close formation, avoid space junk, maximum convoy speed, code gray.' ''

The communications station sends the message, telling the convoy that the situation is touchy but not clear, and also telling the pirates that she is not putting her flotilla on immediate battle alert. In short, she has said, ''All right, all you guys, stay cool!''

Roll two six-sided dice.

If your roll is equal to or less than the fleet's value for Stealth, turn to section 79.

If the roll is greater than the value for Stealth, turn to section 80.

— 79 —

They drift through the passage, the velvet silence broken only by occasional bursts of attitude rockets as a ship adjusts its course or speed.

Emerald draws slow, deep breaths, as if she can maintain control not only of her convoy, but of the dozens of hidden ships surrounding them, by her own will.

"Steady," she hums in a low monotone, as they slip farther and farther into the thick of the enemy. She sees the hands of the duty navigator shaking, with fear or tension. She walks over to his station. He practically jumps out of his seat as he feels her approach.

"Steady," she repeats, this time referring more to him than to the course. He lets out a deep breath and nods his thanks.

"Sure?" she says quietly, raising her eyebrows and looking down at him with all the warmth and support she can project.

"Yes, ma'am. I'm okay."

She nods again and wanders back to her station, for all the world looking as though she is taking a weekend stroll, calm as a clam. Too calm to be believed.

Tension mounts as they start the slow trip out of range of the bandits. Emerald feels the hair on the back of her neck bristle, and a creepy chill shudders down her spine. It's a lot like having someone point a loaded gun at your back. In fact, right now they have a lot of someone pointing a lot of loaded guns. The USJ is an offensive navy with nearly all its ships designed to fire forward. Except for a few gun turrets, and the programmability of smart missiles, they have virtually no firepower to their rear.

"Sitting ducks, aren't we?" the captain comments, leaning over the big screen and mirroring her thoughts.

"I'd love to angle slightly and swing the gun turrets around but that would be an invitation to hit us, and so far they're leaving us be."

"How long until we're effectively out of range?" the captain asks, dropping a hand to Emerald's shoulder. He tries to make it look like a casual gesture, but suddenly he squeezes so hard it hurts. Emerald glances up at Hodges and then traces his gaze to the screen. One of the ships in the unknown fleet is stirring, a big one—maybe as big as the *Inverness*.

"Mr. Phillips, how long?" Emerald relays the question, trying to sound unconcerned.

"About fifteen minutes."

"Longest fifteen minutes of our lives!" the captain whispers, relaxing his grip on her shoulder. She reaches over, puts her hand on his, and squeezes it back. She feels stronger for the companionship of these men and women who share her life, and may yet share her death.

As the chronometer scrolls out the minutes second by second, the electricity in the very air almost crackles. Finally it is over.

"Oh, thank all the powers that be!" Emerald sighs, in a very rare display of open emotion. She slumps, dropping her head to her hands for a moment, delighting in the dancing phosphors she can produce by pressing her palms into her eye sockets. Then she gets up and stretches.

"Coffee's on me." She grins, heading for the pot.

"Coffee, hell." The captain grins, also in a very uncharacteristic gesture. "If we get out of this, I've got a case of Deutscherbrew to share with the entire bridge crew."

A chorus of "Thank you, sir," and "Great!" from officers and crew finally releases the tension of this latest crisis.

Mark off ½ hour from your Time Record Sheet. If this uses up the 12 hours, turn to section 29.

If time remains, turn to section 89.

— 80 —

They drift through the passage, the velvet silence broken only by occasional bursts of attitude rockets as a ship adjusts its course or speed.

Emerald draws slow, deep breaths, as if she can maintain control not only of her convoy, but of the dozens of hidden ships surrounding them, by her own will.

"Steady," she hums in a low monotone, as they slip

farther and farther into the thick of the enemy. She sees the hands of the duty navigator shaking, with fear or tension. She walks over to his station. He practically jumps out of his seat as he feels her approach.

"Steady," she repeats, this time referring more to him than to his course. He lets out a deep breath and nods his thanks.

"Sure?" she says quietly, raising her eyebrows and looking down at him with all the warmth and support she can project.

"Yes, ma'am. I'm okay."

She nods again and wanders back to her station, for all the world looking as though she is taking a weekend stroll, calm as a clam. Too calm to be believed.

But they are reaching the point of no return. Emerald feels the hair on the back of her neck bristle, and a creepy chill shudders down her spine. It felt like having someone point a loaded gun at your back. In fact a lot of someones are pointing a lot of loaded guns. Except for some gun turrets, and the programmability of smart missiles, they are not covered on their rear. The USJ is an "offensive" navy and mounts nearly all of its guns to fire forward.

"Sitting ducks, aren't we?" the captain comments, leaning over the big screen, and mirroring her thoughts.

"I'd love to angle the vector a bit and swing the gun turrets around, but that would be an invitation to hit us, and so far they're leaving us be."

"They're moving in!" Phillips's voice rises to a nerve-shattering shout. On some unheard signal more than two dozen ships in the unknown fleet begin to move at once. The combat monitor glows red, showing every moving ship is armed and ready for combat. Klaxons roar, but every man is already at battle stations and can do nothing but watch as the bandit fleet closes on the naval flotilla. For a brief instant after the alarm stops the bridge is silent.

"Range?" "Status?" The all-too-familiar bulletlike staccato of questions galvanizes the crew to battle readiness.

Emerald is almost relieved, in a bizarre sort of way. Something is happening. The waiting is over.

"Okay, folks," she begins, "the way I see it is this." She is talking to hear her ideas out loud as much as for her junior officers to hear them. She certainly doesn't have time for much input from them.

"We are currently surrounded. Phillips, I want a count and

assessment of their firepower, and I want it yesterday." She spits out the current mission status: number and class of ships remaining, and time left. "Dixon, how are we on ordnance?"

"The supply ship is intact and all ships are carrying a full load. But we can't resupply more than"—Dixon does some quick calculation—"well, the bottom line is that if we want to have anything but rubber bands left to shoot at the Marianas, we have no more than ten full volleys left, at present strength."

"Thank you, Ms. Dixon." Emerald nods at this depressing news. "We've got three choices. We can hold our present configuration and hit them from the 'porcupine.' This gives us the best defense, but it is a static defense, and if we are outgunned and outnumbered we will be picked off one by one. Of course, there is always the possibility we could smear them and take minimal losses this way.

"The second choice is to look for a weak spot, preferably ahead of us, to punch through and make a run for it. The drawback is that we are weak on rear defense. We would be down to a few 360-degree turrets; fewer rear-mounted cannon, and smart missiles, which can be programmed to search and destroy, but if we deploy them we will be depleting ourselves for hitting our primary target, the Marianas fleet.

"The third choice is tricky, and time consuming, but conservative on hardware if we pull it off. They are less likely than we to have rear protection. We can use a standard aerial maneuver from prespace warfare. We can brake as they come up on us, let them fly past, and hit them from the rear. Phillips, how are we doing on enemy strength statistics?"

"Still not finalized, but it looks like they've got thirty ships out there, but mostly old and slow, with minimal firepower."

All this time, Emerald has been scribbling pictures on her lap computer, which she now shows her staff.

"This is what we are going to do," she states, pointing at one of the sketches with her stylus.

Note all the formations mentioned here can be found on the accompanying diagrams.

If you choose to use the porcupine configuration (Choice 1), turn to section 83.

If you choose to cut and run (Choice 2), turn to section 81.

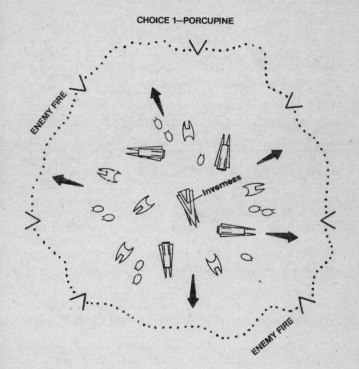

CHOICE 1—PORCUPINE

CHOICE 2—CUT AND RUN

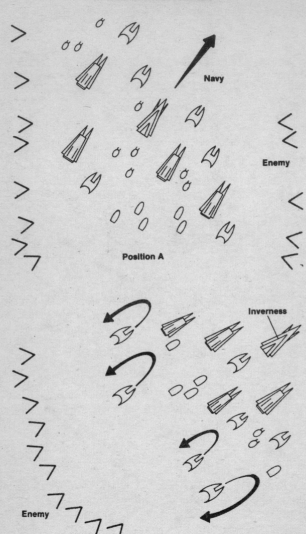

Navy

Enemy

Position A

Inverness

Enemy

Position B

CHOICE 3—BRAKE, RATTLE AND ROLL

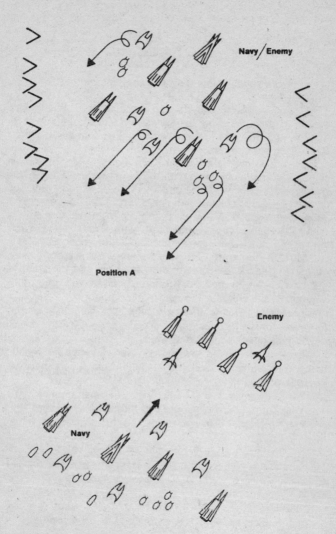

Navy / Enemy

Position A

Enemy

Navy

Position B

If you choose to brake, and try to hit the pirates from the rear (Choice 3), turn to section 82.

— 81 —

Emerald's stylus slams down on the plan calling for them to cut and run.

"Get on the horn to the squad commanders," she orders briskly to Dixon, moving her stylus over the computer screen to show the officer what she wants. "*Nightwing*, out there. *Bear*, drop back to there."

The orders are relayed, and the cruising configuration changed from a stubby ball with the *Inverness* engulfed in the middle, to a cone with the *Inverness* close to the point but covered by the *Nightwing* and her escorts. The rear is packed with vessels that can deliver firepower from the rear, those with 360-degree gun turrets, rear guns, and at least one destroyer-escort with torpedo tubes and antitorpedo missiles.

"Move it, move it!" Emerald shouts at the screen, urging on her flotilla as the configuration finalizes and the engines gun to maximum gee. "Afterburner city, you good-for-nothings!" she continued in her tirade, tapping her stylus in a rapid staccato. She is slammed back into her chair as the *Inverness* thrusts into maximum speed.

The hull rattles time and again as the cruiser takes dozens of direct hits from the low-power laser cannons and small-bore explosive shells volleyed at them from the corridor of pirate ships.

"We're through. We're clear," the radarman chimes.

"Yes, but they're behind us, and they aren't leaving."

"Fire on them," Emerald snaps. "What's our range? Are they closing?"

"No, ma'am, we are pulling ahead, but slowly."

Dixon leans over to Phillips and asks, in parody of the old relativity question, "Do we have enough speed to outrun our shells?"

"Doesn't matter," he whispers back. "The enemy is going to run into them twice as fast as we fired them!" They grin at each other.

The enemy can fire on Emerald's flotilla with only 15 ships and not the cruiser, each firing with an Ordnance Value of 3 (Attack Strength initially 45). The rest of their fleet is out of range or position. The pirates fire using Chart D.

Emerald can fire on the enemy with only half her ships each round, (round upward if you have an odd number). They fire using Chart D.

After 3 exchanges the unknown fleet will break off as Emerald's flotilla pulls away.

If Emerald has lost, or does not have 5 or more ships left, turn to section 29.

If Emerald survives with the Inverness *and 5 more ships, turn to section 84.*

Unknown Fleet:

Type	Ordnance value
Cruiser	6*
Destroyer	3
Escort 1	3
Escort 2	3
Escort 3	3
Bird 1	3
Bird 2	3
Converted Merchant	3
Converted Merchant	3
Converted Merchant	3
Converted Merchant	3
Converted Merchant	3
Converted Merchant	3
Converted Merchant	3
Converted Merchant	3
Converted Merchant	3
Converted Merchant	3
Converted Merchant	3
Converted Merchant	3
Converted Merchant	3
Converted Merchant	3

Type	Ordnance value
Converted Merchant	3
Converted Merchant	3
Converted Merchant	3
Converted Merchant	3
Converted Tender	3
Converted Tanker	3
Converted Tug	3
Converted Tug	3

*This ship counts as two when computing attack value, but is destroyed by one hit.

— 82 —

Emerald slams her stylus down on the plan for the braking maneuver.

Captain Hodges is wearing his worried look again. "Timing this is going to be touchy, Emerald. This was designed for single-plane dogfighters."

"I know, Brad. Believe me, I know. But if we can stuff it up their tubes, we've got them."

"I'm game. Let's do it." He smiles, and she smiles back, again having reason to appreciate her fellow officer.

"Dixon, send this in code to the squad leaders." She rattles off the code book numbers that will execute this maneuver, then adds, "At negative two gees, and repeat that." She is praying that she doesn't have to get on the horn and explain this in plain language.

The plan is not only to brake, but to avoid being rear-ended by stray enemy ships that pass through, while avoiding enemy fire the whole time. To do this, Emerald has ordered a very stressful maneuver called a controlled tumble, much like its counterpart performed in atmosphere.

"Initiate sequence. Fire attitude rockets. Reverse thrust engines activated. Ten, nine, eight. Power at seventy-eight percent. Four, three, two, one. Fire."

The sudden jolt which follows the wild spin knocks bodies into restraining straps with bone-snapping suddenness. It also turns the most reckless jock on board into a white-knuckled passenger.

Emerald monitors her output, fighting the bucking ship and the pain in her joints.

"We're rocking tonight," she shouts, as she sees her entire complement of ships dropping behind the enemy and stabilizing with the precision of a chorus line.

"Awesome!" she shouts, her heart pounding. "Get them into position."

Dixon relays the next order. The flotilla drops into the shape of a contact lens, forming a three-dimensional crescent around the rear of the enemy fleet.

"Mop them up!" Emerald orders.

The squad leaders issue orders to their escorts, and targets are assigned. It's like shooting fish in a barrel. But after two volleys, the enemy has also reconfigured and is shooting back.

The USJ does not count any drones in your ship total; any remaining are being saved for the flanking attack. Therefore any remaining drones are secured to the tugs. The fleet fires using Chart B. Emerald may fire 3 rounds without return fire before the enemy can reposition for its first combat round.

The pirates start with 30 ships. They fire with an Ordnance Value of 3 each. Furthermore, they only have enough ammo for 8 exchanges. If they survive that long, they will break off and run away. They fire using Chart E.

If Emerald loses, or if she wins but is reduced to fewer than five ships including the Inverness, *turn to section 29.*

If Emerald wins, turn to section 86.

Unknown Pirate Fleet.

Type	Ordnance value
Cruiser	6*
Destroyer	3
Escort 1	3
Escort 2	3
Escort 3	3
Bird 1	3

Type	Ordnance value
Bird 2	3
Converted Merchant	3
Converted Merchant	3
Converted Merchant	3
Converted Merchant	3
Converted Merchant	3
Converted Merchant	3
Converted Merchant	3
Converted Merchant	3
Converted Merchant	3
Converted Merchant	3
Converted Merchant	3
Converted Merchant	3
Converted Merchant	3
Converted Merchant	3
Converted Merchant	3
Converted Merchant	3
Converted Merchant	3
Converted Merchant	3
Converted Merchant	3
Converted Tender	3
Converted Tanker	3
Converted Tug	3
Converted Tug	3

— 83 —

Emerald's stylus slams down on the diagram of the porcupine formation.

"Circle the wagons, Mr. Phillips," she orders, winking at him.

He grins as he issues the orders. The running gag has some teeth. The navy really is on the untamed frontier out here, and the pirates are as rough and ruthless as any army of aborigines in the Wild West on Terra.

The *Inverness* is not taking the brunt of the assault, as she is enveloped by the protection of her escort. But she has a lot of heavy firepower that is going to waste.

"Brad," Emerald confers quietly with the captain, "can we find a slot to shoot through? A safe one?"

"Yes, I think I can do that." He orders a course change for the *Inverness*, and now she is leveling her laser cannon at the tubes of a ragged Solar War I destroyer.

At a gunnery station on a deck below, a gunner's mate locks his weapon on the enemy.

"Beam away!" he yells as the gun crew scrambles for handholds. The big gun fires, sending shock waves through the gunnery section.

"Check power load," the mate shouts.

"Power full," comes the trained reply.

"Tracking target. Target locked. Beam away!"

The crew scrambles again for their stations and another pirate ship is history.

Another form of the kata of war is being danced in the missile section. The ordnance officer is listening to the bridge fire-control coordinator for orders, pressing his ear-jack hard to hear over the noise on deck. Antitorp missiles, and torpedoes themselves, are not to be used without direct orders from the bridge. They will be too necessary in the final assault on the Marianas fleet to be wasted on this trash, unless it can't be helped.

"What? I do not copy," he shouts into the pickup.

The voice in the officer's ear is little more than white noise. "Damn laser cannon," he mutters. The big gun blows ship communication each time it recharges. The voice from the bridge clears as the power drain drops. ". . . heavy cruiser, bearing . . ."

"I copy." The missile officer shouts the data to his mate. A heavy cruiser, of the *Independence* class, a late model from Solar War II, is in range, and they have locked a torpedo on the *Inverness*. The telemetry on the missile deck shows the older cruiser's profile as she launches at the *Inverness*.

"Missile targeted and locked. Missile away," the gunnery officer announces in one breath.

The sleek cylinder arcs and swerves away from the *Inverness* as it plots its own course to the torpedo.

The *Inverness* rocks with the shock wave as the torpedo is detonated in space, far too close for the comfort of Captain Hodges.

"Nuke that thing!" he orders, pointing his finger at the image of the cruiser on the screen.

The word goes down the line. A heavy smart torpedo is launched and locks on the cruiser. It scores a direct hit, but the old cruiser is far from dead in the water, although its hull is breached. They made them sturdy for that war. Internal bulkheads reseal the ship, although the debris, some of it organic, can be seen drifting from a huge hole in the aft section.

"Fire two."

Another smart torpedo stalks its prey and scores another hit. The laser cannon finishes the job, blasting through the torpedo hole before the enemy vessel can secure its interior. The beam spews out the far side of the pirate cruiser, then dances jaggedly over her few remaining intact sections of hull.

The missile officer again presses the jack to his ear. "What was that?" he shouts, muttering, "Damn lasers," to himself. "Oh, thank you, sir." He conveys the "well done" to his crew.

On the bridge, Emerald paces back and forth from station to station, scanning screens and output, reaching out to steady herself as the vessel bucks and pitches with near-misses and small but jolting direct hits.

"*Nightwing*," she orders her squad leader aboard the destroyer, "bring your escorts around to port. Pull in. We're too thin in your sector. *Bear*, your birds are bunching up. Let 'em out a little. More. Still more. Good," she orders watching the pattern on her screen. "*Nightwing*, you've got a bogey at twelve o'clock." She watches anxiously until the pirate's blip winks out.

Exclude drones from the total of ships; these are currently reattached to their tugs, if any remain. You fire using Chart C.

The pirates fire with an Ordnance Value of 3 each. They fire using Chart E.

The pirates do not have an unlimited number of shells, either. After 8 rounds, if any pirates are left, Emerald gets 2 free shots at them. After this tenth round, the remaining combatants, if any, break off the fight. If, at the end of combat, Emerald's flotilla is totally destroyed, or has fewer than 5 ships, turn to section 88.

If *Emerald* destroys or drives off the pirate fleet and *has five or more ships remaining, turn to section 87.*

Unknown Pirate Fleet:

Type	Ordnance value
Cruiser	6*
Destroyer	3
Escort 1	3
Escort 2	3
Escort 3	3
Bird 1	3
Bird 2	3
Converted Merchant	3
Converted Merchant	3
Converted Merchant	3
Converted Merchant	3
Converted Merchant	3
Converted Merchant	3
Converted Merchant	3
Converted Merchant	3
Converted Merchant	3
Converted Merchant	3
Converted Merchant	3
Converted Merchant	3
Converted Merchant	3
Converted Merchant	3
Converted Merchant	3
Converted Merchant	3
Converted Merchant	3
Converted Merchant	3
Converted Tender	3
Converted Tanker	3
Converted Tug	3
Converted Tug	3

*This ship counts as two when computing attack value, but is destroyed by one hit.

— 84 —

"Status report," Emerald commands, sinking down into her chair.

Her command crew sing out the damage reports as the squad leaders report in. All in all, they have survived another one. But they are all getting a little ragged around the edges. Emerald wonders just how much more her flotilla will have to take before they make their rendezvous, *if* they make it, and if they will be in any shape to fight when they get there.

Cross ½ hour off the Time Record Sheet.

If all twelve hours have passed, turn to section 29. If they have not, turn to section 85.

— 85 —

Some of the ships are damaged but not destroyed. If you feel you have time to stop and effect repairs, you may do so.

If you wish to make repairs, roll one six-sided die. If you roll 4 or less, you have completed repairs on any 2 ships and lost 1 hour. If you have rolled a 5 or 6, the ships you tried to fix are beyond repair. If you wish, you may roll again, docking yourself 1 hour for every roll, as long as you wish, until you are back up to the number of ships with which you began this engagement. When you are finished, turn to section 89.

— 86 —

At a gunnery station on a deck below, a gunner's mate locks his weapon on the enemy.

"Beam away!" he yells as the gun crew scrambles for handholds. The big gun fires, sending shock waves through the gunnery section.

"Check power load," the mate shouts.

"Power full," comes the trained reply.

"Tracking target. Target locked. Beam away!"

The crew scrambles again for their stations and another pirate ship is history.

Another form of the kata of war is being danced in the missile section. The ordnance officer is listening to the bridge fire-control coordinator for orders, pressing his ear-jack hard into his ear to hear over the noise on deck. Antitorp missiles, and torpedos themselves, are not to be used without direct orders from the bridge. They will be too necessary in the final assault on the Marianas fleet to be wasted on this trash, unless it can't be helped.

"What? I do not copy," he shouts into the pickup.

The voice in the officer's ear is little more than white noise. "Damn laser cannon," he mutters. The big gun blows ship communication each time it recharges. The voice from the bridge clears as the power drain drops. ". . . heavy cruiser, bearing . . ."

"I copy." The missile officer shouts the data to his mate. A heavy cruiser, of the *Independence* class, a late model from Solar War II, is in range, and they have locked a torpedo on the *Inverness*. The telemetry on the missile deck shows it as it launches.

"Missile targeted and locked. Missile away."

The sleek cylinder arcs and swerves away from the *Inverness* as it plots its own course to the torpedo.

The *Inverness* rocks with the shock wave as the torpedo is detonated in space, but far too close for the comfort of Captain Hodges.

"Nuke that thing!" he orders, pointing his finger at the image of the cruiser on the screen.

The word goes down the line. A heavy smart torpedo is launched and locks on the cruiser. It scores a direct hit, but the cruiser is far from dead in the water, although its hull is breached. Internal bulkheads reseal the ship, although the debris, some of it organic, can be seen drifting from a huge hole in the aft section.

"Fire two."

Another smart torpedo stalks its prey and scores another hit. The laser cannon finishes the job, blasting through the torpedo hole before the enemy vessel can secure its interior.

The missile officer again presses the jack to his ear. "What was that?" he shouts, muttering, "Damn lasers," to himself. "Oh, thank you, sir." He conveys the "well done" to his crew.

The crew has got in some good hits, and the morale is up when Emerald issues the order to stand down.

Add a point to Morale, but there is one problem. This maneuver has caused a serious power drain and took a lot of time. You have lost 1 hour. Mark this off on your time sheet. If your time has just been reduced to zero, turn to section 29.

If not, just subtract 1 hour from your time chart and turn to section 85.

— 87 —

The assault seems endless, but attrition is on Emerald's side, and after what seems like forever, the order to stand down is given.

You have lost 1½ hours. Mark this off on your time sheet. If you are now out of time, turn to section 29.

If you still have time, turn to section 85.

— 88 —

The assault seems endless, but attrition is on Emerald's side. She is just beginning to allow herself to think ahead to the stand-down order, when she hears Phillips mutter, "Oh, Jesus Christ!"

The crack in his voice is a warning as loud as a scream. Emerald turns and scans his screen. A new blip is moving in and closing fast. Before she can ask, Phillips has put it on visual.

"Oh, no," she says lamely. She puts out the order to hit it with everything they've got, but she knows nothing will help. Cruising into firing range is a *Potemkin*-class battleship, armed with the latest and best guns and missiles the Saturnian navy has to sell. The ship is flying the colors of an ally to the Saturnian block, known terrorists who consider themselves at open war with the USJ.

The battleship opens fire on Emerald's depleted flotilla. The *Inverness* receives a direct hit to the engine room. It is over before they can abandon ship.

Turn to section 29.

— 89 —

"Status report," Emerald barks.

Dixon gives her the latest figures, and the bridge crew's best guess on how long to rendezvous. It's not that they don't know where they are; they don't know how fast they can safely proceed. Even though this section of space is a super-highway compared to the surrounding sand trap, they don't have what anybody would call clear sailing. And the last little surprise makes Emerald wonder just how alone they are out here.

Her fears are realized when Phillips, looking very puzzled, says, "Ma'am, would you take a look at this?"

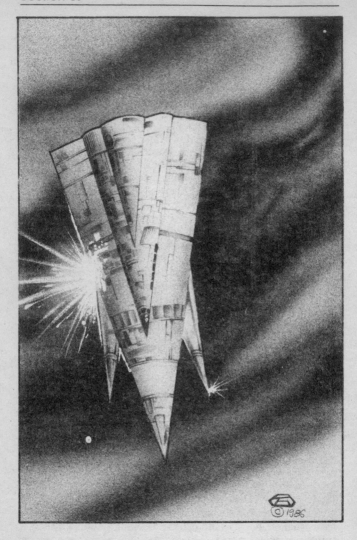

© 1986

"Patch it over to me," Emerald orders, unsure that she has the strength to get up out of her seat.

"I'd rather, if you don't mind, ma'am . . ." Phillips replies, fidgeting with embarrassment and tugging on his ear.

Emerald raises her eyebrows and shrugs, as she struggles to her feet and walks over the Phillips, wondering if he has, over the years, actually tugged those elephant ears of his out to their exaggerated size by pulling on them.

"Yes, what is it?" she says testily, unaccustomed to being summoned by subordinates.

"Well, I'm not sure, but it doesn't look right." He has a visual display of the sector directly ahead of the flotilla on his screen. Above and slightly to the right there is a large object, an asteroid about twice the size of a battleship, which appears to be chugging right along with them.

"It's not only the movement, ma'am, it just isn't dense enough for an asteroid, even if it were an ice chunk. I think it's a disguised or discarded bubble."

Emerald thinks back to the refugee bubbles she has heard about. The bubble is the most common form of stable environmental unit in her solar system, large ones providing accommodation for almost all human habitation, farming, and industry. The small ones are utilized as cheap, slow transport, for cargo, and for thousands of political refugees from the minority nations—people. These relatively helpless and unarmed vehicles have been the primary target for the piratical activities that have grown to plague the spaceways from the Belt clear to the Saturn sector, and probably beyond.

In fact, the only reason that Emerald's task force has had any modicum of success in stabilizing the peace is that the pirates themselves have organized into pseudo-nations and armies in an attempt to solidify control. In doing so, however, at least some of them have become like the settled middle-class businessmen they make their fortunes preying upon. The navy's treaty with the notorious pirate leader named Straight, sealed by Captain Hope Hubris's marriage to Straight's daughter, was the proof of that.

The more Emerald stares at the object that has temporarily joined their convoy, the more she is sure that it isn't natural. Into Emerald's mind crowd images of boarding it and finding the skeletons of refugees whose dreams of freedom ended in death.

"Yeah, Phillips, it's what you think it is. Just keep an eye on it. Sparks, would you please listen to that object over there. See if you can detect anybody on board. Dixon, monitor for bioactivity readouts.''

Emerald really hasn't the time to stop and rescue a bunch of dead people, if that is what they are. Its hull appears to be intact, and the camouflage seems to be not only natural, in the form of adherent ice and debris, but an improvement on nature.

"Ma'am, we have life readings on board. Quite a number," Dixon reports.

"Let's check in on them. Open a hailing frequency. Lie a little. Make us a survey ship. And keep the beam tight."

"USJ survey vessel *Inverness* to unidentified bubble, come in please. They are not answering, ma'am."

"Keep it up."

"Yes, ma'am."

"Maybe we should just leave them alone, but I'm liable to have nightmares about abandoning some dying survivors if we don't check it out. Tell them to answer or we board."

The radioman transmits the warning, then says, "Wait, I've got an answer."

"Put it through."

Scratchy sound fills the bridge, and a fuzzy picture appears on her screen. The man is a middle-aged fellow, with a straggly beard, wearing dozens of strings of small beads. He is not wearing much else.

"We are well. Go in peace," he intones.

The transmission blinks out.

"Ma'am, could it be one of those cults?" Dixon asks.

"Could be. What did you have in mind?"

"Well, I read something somewhere about those back-to-nature groups who wanted to live like the ancient earth aborigines, usually with some religious guru behind them. They get a bubble and just take off. Some of these groups die off or quit, but there must still be dozens of them living off their own land and minding their own business."

"Possible. I guess they have their rights."

"Rights!" The bitterness of the voice grabs not only Emerald's attention but the attention of most of the bridge crew.

"Spaceman?" the captain asks.

"Sorry, sir. That was out of line." But the crewman is still scowling at his console, and his back is as rigid as a board.

"What is it, Rhodes?" the captain asks, genuine concern creasing his face.

"Well, sir, I was born on one of those damn cult bubbles. They were nuts. Even as a kid I knew that. Well, that's not fair, either, but there were a lot of us who hated it. They were real mean, although they talked about how much they loved us. Wanted to beat evil out of everybody, but I noticed when I was still pretty young that women and children got beat a lot more often than men. Anyhow, my sister and I escaped when the bubble had to dock for repairs. They tried to get us back but we were real lucky. USJ judge said we could stay, and then he ordered an investigation of the whole bubble. But we were just lucky."

"If we lose them, there's a chance we'll never find them again, but we're on a mission," Emerald says, almost to herself. "Damn it, where're all these damn people coming from? The belt is supposed to be thinly settled, but we're bumping into more people than New Manhattan Dome at lunchtime. Still, we have to do something. Can we tag it?"

"Yes, ma'am," Rhodes says, brightening. "I can target a beacon on them so gentle, it will land like talc on a baby."

"Good, set it up to begin transmitting by a naval code signal trigger. That way they won't be broadcasting a big 'Eat at Joe's' for every stray pirate, but we can find them again when we've got the time. I'll put it to Captain Hubris when we complete the mission. He's a real sucker for refugees."

"Thank you, ma'am," Rhodes says. The catch in his voice tells how close he is to tears.

He sends the tiny probe out to lodge itself on the hull of the colony with the anonymity of a piece of stray space dust. The flotilla moves on.

"Come on, Emerald, it's time to eat . . . real food." The captain takes her by the arm and steers her toward the wardroom, shouting, "You've got the conn," to his exec over his shoulder as he leaves.

He browses around in the refer, muttering something about tacos.

"How about Mexican food?" he asks Emerald.

"I don't think I could—"

"Well, kid, it's that or Salisbury steak. Let's see, we've got an enchilada of sorts, a fake burrito, and a heap of rice and beans. Hey, it's even got . . . apple pie! There's your basic Mexican dessert.'' He sticks two of the frozen dinners in the microwave and fetches two packs of milk.

"It's some kind of bloody circus out there, Emerald," Brad sighs, handing her a straw for her milk.

"No lie!" She grins. "So much for our quiet little cruise."

"The actual battle is going to be a piece of cake after this! There." He gets up as a bell on the microwave rings. "Swill's on!"

She laughs a little too loudly, and then the laugh becomes a flood of tears.

The captain brings the steaming tray to the table, settles back, and lets her get it all out.

"Oh, God, I feel so dumb," she says, wiping the tears away. "But I also feel a heap better. And hungry."

She wolfs into the chow, dispatching it with amazing speed. The captain watches her, smiling slightly, not far behind her in the chow-down department.

"Oh, wow! Thanks, Brad."

"No sweat." They sit for a moment, savoring the quiet and familiarity of the dull room, its steel-framed tables topped with undistinguished gray-blue plastic, the slightly tattered upholstery on the couch against the wall, the rack with the few out-of-date magazines and videotapes.

"We're doing good, aren't we?" Emerald asks.

"We're still alive, and we're still cruising, aren't we?" Hodges replies, countering with another question.

"Yeah, you're right. Back to reality?"

Brad guffaws. "Some reality! I'll lay you odds we're going to run into two-headed green-tentacled aliens within ten minutes!"

"No bet, smartass. Let's go."

The break has perked them both up. Emerald files a wonderful new notion in the back of her head. Tough or not tough, commanders who are starving and falling off their feet aren't much use to anybody.

"How goes it, Dixon?"

"Steady."

"Good."

It is actually more like twenty minutes and it is no green-tentacled alien, but another damn privateer.

"Hail, milady." The carefully groomed, bewhiskered, and costumed man leers out at Emerald from the screen.

"Oh, Christ, another nut case!" Emerald says loudly and

clearly. The man's leer turns into a twisted grimace. Emerald pursues her advantage. "Stand down and surrender. You have exactly thirty seconds. Failure to comply will result in your immediate and total destruction." She slams her communication button and the man's face fades from the screen.

"Oh, God, I hate these geeks. Captain Kidd, my ass! What does this jerk call himself?"

Phillips goes red all over as he says, "Big Hairy Dick!"

Emerald throws back her head and roars, joined by her comrades. "Okay, that's it." She opens the channel and snaps, "Your time is up."

"So is yours. I have a planet-buster locked onto your position."

"He does," Dixon whispers.

"If you hit me, my convoy will vaporize you. Don't tell me you're that dumb. Crazy maybe, but dumb?"

"These are my terms, sweet one!" He grins in triumph. "Single combat, you and me. You win, you live and I leave. You lose, you live with me and I get your ship."

Out of voice range, Emerald is shaking her head in amazement. "I don't believe this guy." Then she returns to her console. "Give me a minute to consult with my staff."

"You have thirty seconds," he spits out, grinning.

"We have no choice," Emerald states flatly.

"Can you take him?" asks Captain Hodges, with real concern.

"A bigger question is can we take the time? Guess there's no choice. He's big, but cocky. He'll strut in and rush and make a mistake. I can take him."

"This is crazy," the captain mutters, shaking his head.

"Okay, you're on," Emerald says to the fop on the screen. "Your challenge, so my weapons. Knives, to the death."

"Don't worry, my ebon lovely. I shall spare you."

"Well, folks," she says to her staff, after the arrangements for time and place have been made, "let's stack the deck. This ain't no game, no matter what that lunkhead thinks."

Emerald quickly confers with the captain and Phillips. Then she says, "Come on, Dixon, let's get me ready."

They jog down to their quarters, where Emerald rummages in her bag. "It's here somewhere. Aha!" She triumphantly pulls out a small laser gun. It is barely two inches long and an inch wide. The battery holds enough charges for only two shots. "Don't really like these lady guns, but it was a gift. I carry it mostly for luck.'' She drops her belt and pulls free her holster and standard-issue side arm.

"I'm not sure I understand," Dixon says, staring at the laser. "You gave your word, and you did say you could take him."

"And my word is good, Dixon," Emerald snaps as she tucks the gun in a sleeve, "as long as my opponent keeps *his* word. If he comes prepared for single combat, knives only, that's what he'll get. But if he tries anything funny, I'm bound—honor bound, to Captain Hubris and the task force—to be prepared. As extra insurance, I've arranged that if the pirate breaks his word, Captain Hodges is to blast the platform we are fighting on and then nuke the pirate ship. Our pirate friend has promised to disarm the planet-buster before we fight, not that I believe him. But it's what we've got to work with."

As she heads for the shuttle that will take her to the pirate's landing craft, which is to be used for the combat platform, a group of three Slugs approach her in the passageway.

"Ma'am. Excuse me, ma'am. We were wondering if you would . . ." One of the Slugs reverently hands her his sheathed Slug commando knife. She looks at the man and reaches out to touch the weapon. His square jaw is pulled in tight to where a lesser man's neck would be.

"I'd be honored, commando."

"If there is any way you could let one of us—"

"I don't doubt the greenest rookie among you could turn this jerk into hamburger, but I'm stuck with it. On the other hand, my black belt is as black as any man jack's among you." She grins, takes the knife and tucks it into her belt, removing the navy-issue weapon she wore and handing it to Dixon.

"Thanks," she says to the commando, just a little embarrassed and punching him in the arm as she passes to cover her discomfort. The man grins back and salutes as she leaves, but she can hear them shout, "Go, Commander Sheller," "Go for it, Emerald," "Kiss ass, ma'am," as she dogtrots down the hall.

She dons her vacuum suit, slipping the scabbard with the knife onto her utility belt and tucking the gun out of sight in her left glove. Two spacemen are aboard the shuttle, the pilot and the navigator. That both of them are third-degree black belts in karate, one of them having equal honors in judo and the other a weapons teacher, is not coincidental, she suspects, smiling at Hodges. Emerald gestures a thumbs-up and they roar off to the landing craft.

The buccaneer and his seconds are already on board. Emerald stifles a laugh when she sees her opponent. He has managed to pad his vacuum suit to bulge in a most protective way. *Maybe he's a bit worried about having something vital cut off,* she muses to herself. Big Hairy Dick seems annoyed at her amusement. Evidently she is supposed to be terrified. Maybe if she was one of those cadets they are graduating now, she would be. Emerald meets his eyes and then scans his companions. The two men with him are large and mean-eyed. The type you expect to start fights in bars.

"I thought we were to fight alone," Emerald chides. "Are you afraid of being alone with a woman?"

"Get out!" the pirate bellows to his men. Emerald gestures for her men to leave also.

"But, Captain, we were going to search her," one of the pirates whines, hesitating at the hatch.

Roll two six-sided dice.

If the number rolled is the same as or less than the value for the fleet's Morale, turn to section 90.

If it is greater than the value for Morale, turn to section 91.

— 90 —

"I said get out!" Dick bellows.

Emerald doesn't twitch as the various seconds leave the vessel.

"Shall I do the honors?" she asks with exaggerated courtesy, walking over to the control panel at the aft of the small craft.

"As you wish, milady," Dick answers, with a ridiculous flourish.

Emerald turns to reach for the controls that will evacuate the air from the boat, and will also dampen the gravity. This is to be a free-fall fight, one in which any rip to a pressure suit causes instant death.

"By the way, you did honor our agreement to disarm the bomb, didn't you?" Emerald asks. She turns her head to see the pirate has a laser pistol pointed directly at her.

"Bomb?" the pirate replies in mock surprise. "Oh, that bomb. It must have slipped my mind."

"I thought it might," she says, turning full toward him as the tiny gun appears in her hand, and without further conversation her laser tears his chest into a splattered mass of blood and scorched flesh. Big Dick drops, shock still evident on his face. Commander Sheller makes a brief note to be more tolerant of chauvinists; it slows their reflexes.

As she opens a radio channel on her helmet transmitter, she thinks how grateful she is that they are not in zero gee. The mess on the floor is bad enough.

When the *Inverness* acknowledges her signal, she says, "Melt them. And get me out of here!"

The next few seconds are crucial. The shuttle is defenseless and if the *Inverness* gives them the chance, the pirate ship's smallest cannon will tear it apart. Emerald paces, impatiently awaiting her shuttle, and finally hears the thud of a vessel docking. The panel slides open, and two pirate goons come tumbling in. They must have seen their ship destroyed and come back for revenge. It does not take her long to go into combat mode. Sheller blasts the first with the last charge in her pistol. He crumples in the doorway. The second pirate dodges past the shot, and leaps for her. She sidesteps him, powering a blow to the back of his neck as he goes by. It hardly slows him as he stumbles back up to his feet and charges her again. He is a bull of a man with a neck as thick as his head, standing a head taller than the USJ officer.

Emerald has the knife in her hand, and she slashes up toward his throat. She rips into fabric, but the little ship is still pressurized. And a good thing, because he, too, has drawn a weapon, a saber from somewhere inside his massive vacsuit. He cuts at her, slashing at her belly with the first cut and back across her face with the second. She steps out of range, then sweeps her arm up, parrying away the flat of his blade with her forearm, and charges up below the blade, driving her knife into his throat. There is a trickle of blood where the edge of the saber cut into her arms. It stings more than hurts.

"Commander, Commander." The pilot of her shuttle comes running in. They have managed to board by docking to the pirate ship, a sloppy maneuver at best, but the only way in.

"What took you guys so long?" Emerald pants out. But she gratefully accepts their offer to be helped aboard her own vessel. Suddenly she feels a bit weak-kneed. She decides she just didn't need this after two space battles and a spy.

Meanwhile, aboard the *Inverness*, Captain Hodges has issued the order for destruction of the pirate vessel.

"They're firing on us, sir. Their bomb. It's still operational and locked on target. They can launch amidships in a few seconds, probably kill us both."

"Bring the main battery to bear amidships. Fire at will," he orders the gunnery deck, muttering to himself, "If they're space dust they can't launch a bomb."

Roll two six-sided dice.

If the number rolled is equal to or less than the value for Morale, turn to section 92.

If it is greater than the value for Morale, turn to section 93.

— 91 —

"*I'll* search her good," Dick says with a leer, "after I've pulled her teeth. And I don't mind an audience while I do it."

Before Emerald can issue any orders to her escort, the pirate captain rushes toward her, his knife held low in his right hand, his left arm up in guard position.

It doesn't take Emerald long to go into combat mode. The commando knife appears in her hand, and she closes with him to slash upward toward his throat. Her speed gets her past his guard, and the knife rips into the fabric of his suit. But the little ship is still pressurized, so the blow is not fatal.

Before she can disengage, he cuts at her, slashing at her belly with the first arc and back across her face with the second. Again, Emerald's greater speed gives her the advantage. She steps out of range, then sweeps her arm up, parrying away the flat of his blade. Without losing momentum, she charges in to drive her knife into the pirate's throat. A thin trickle of blood begins to seep through a slash in her vacsuit's arm.

As he slumps to the deck, one of his two goons pulls a heavy-charge side arm. The shuttle pilot kicks the weapon out of his hand and it spins to the deck near Emerald. She grabs for it, but the second goon jumps at her. She rolls out of his way, but he grabs the weapon.

She rolls again, just in time to keep from being fried. The pilot smashes down on Goon Number One's neck with a knife strike, crushing the windpipe. Holding the dying pirate for a shield, he turns to face the armed Goon Number Two. The trouble is the next exchange of fire is likely to breach the hull and kill them all.

By now, all three naval officers are standing, ready to dodge or strike, the armed pirate crouched in their midst. Emerald is holding her mini-laser centered on his head.

I'll bet these guys play kickball, Emerald thinks.

"Okay, Creighton," she says to the navigator, whose name is Jones, "Brown has the ball."

The radiant look of comprehension that washes over his face is a joy Emerald will never forget. "Got'cha, Radcliffe," he sings out.

He fakes left and dodges right, the pilot "passing" the now-dead goon as a distraction to the left flank. Emerald circles behind to the far right, leaving the armed pirate waving his gun back and forth from one to the other.

"Here," Emerald shouts, sending the man spinning around toward her. As he does, the weapons expert makes a lightning-fast pass, grabbing the man's arm and forcing it up. He twists it back, the powerful pistol discharging into one of the shuttle's seats. Then it is finished, and the pirate is sprawled on the deck, his neck bent at an odd angle.

"What took you guys so long?" Emerald pants out. "The Cougars mopped the Miners in half the time."

Their laughter turns the adventure into instant "war stories." It's their way of offering each other deserved congratulations. The laughter continues to help them unwind from the tense adrenaline high as they fly the shuttle back to the *Inverness*.

Meanwhile, aboard the *Inverness*, Captain Hodges has issued the order for destruction of the pirate vessel.

"They're firing on us, sir. Their bomb. It's still operational and locked on target. It can be launched amidships in seconds. Blow the whole fleet to hell.''

"Bring the main battery to bear amidships. Fire at will," Hodges orders the gunnery deck, muttering to himself, "If they're space dust, they can't launch a bomb.''

Roll two six-sided dice.

If the number rolled is equal to or less than the value for Morale, turn to section 92.

If it is greater than the value for Morale, turn to section 93.

— 92 —

The navy levels everything it has on the one small but dangerous ship, which still hasn't launched its big bomb. As Emerald's shuttle docks with the *Inverness*, she speculates on whether it is in respect for the promise made by Dead Dick or, more likely, if the crew is unable to launch the bomb. They may be lacking the technical know-how or, even more likely, be busy fighting for position among themselves, now that the captaincy is vacant.

She braces herself against the bulkhead as the laser cannon blasts, its vibration shaking the entire ship.

By the time she arrives at the bridge, it is over. The *Inverness* has shot the pirate ship out of space without receiving any serious return fire, except for totally inadequate shelling.

Responding to the hopeful looks of several of her fellow officers, Emerald laughs, "I'll tell you about it later. Let's get out of here."

Cross ½ hour off the time record, and if there is time left, turn to section 94.

— 93 —

The navy levels everything it has on the one small but dangerous ship, which still hasn't launched its big bomb. As Emerald's shuttle docks with the *Inverness*, she speculates on whether it is in respect for the promise made by Dead Dick or, more likely, if the crew is unable to launch the bomb. They may be lacking the technical know-how or, even more likely, be busy fighting for position among themselves, now that the captaincy is vacant.

She braces herself against the bulkhead as the laser cannon blasts, its vibration shaking the entire ship. She breaks into a dead run as soon as she can, and heads for the bridge.

"Status," she shouts as she bullets in. But she shuts up as she assesses the situation.

"They have launched," Captain Hodges says quietly.

The antitorp crews have the bomb in their sights as soon as it appears. It's going to be touch and go. The missiles must destroy the bomb before it gets so close to the *Inverness* that exploding the torpedo will destroy the naval flagship, too.

Hodges screams for evasive maneuvers. Around them the other ships scatter, firing at the missile as they withdraw. A stray shot from the cruiser's main battery misses the missile, but slams squarely into the lone pirate ship that launched it. The enemy vessel is a lifeless hulk even before the massive missile completes its course toward the *Inverness*.

The bomb has an Attack Strength of 50, and will have only one combat roll. Use Chart E for the bomb's attack.

The navy fires first, using Chart F. If the navy scores a hit, the bomb is destroyed. If they do not and the bomb strikes a hit in its half of the round, the Inverness *will be destroyed. If the* Inverness *is destroyed, turn to section 29.*

If the navy destroys it or the bomb also misses, cross 1 hour off your time record and, if there is time left, turn to section 94.

— 94 —

"I just don't know where these creeps come from, Brad."
Emerald is sitting in the sickbay having the cut on her arm
and a couple of cuts and scrapes that had gone unnoticed in
the excitement tended to. The captain leans against an examination
table and sips a cola.

"I've read a couple of pop psychology theories about it,"
Emerald continues. "I mean, I know a lot of guys who spend
their free time in Japanese fighting clothes doing ancient and
venerable things, and I know a few who spend their free time
in Solar War I clubs and the like, and that's all pretty healthy.
Hell, I used to dress up in costume and juggle for street fairs
and summer festivals when I was in high school. It was fun.
But these guys, do they really think they're eighteenth-century
Earth pirates?" Emerald asks.

Brad shakes his head. "Beats me. I can understand, in a
way. Look, if you don't make it in something larger than life,
like the military or the government, and you want something—
something special—where is there to get it anymore? The city
bubbles are crowded, and there isn't much opportunity to be a
music or video star for all those fame-starved kids. So the
sane ones head for the frontier, and the crazy ones delude
themselves into thinking they are Blackbeard the Pirate. But
I'm no expert," the captain finishes.

"That one was kind of funny, in a sick way," Emerald
laughs ruefully. "Do you know, he had a codpiece on his
vacuum suit. It was so stuffed, I don't know how he could
walk. Honest!"

Emerald hops off the table, fastens her jumpsuit, and squares
her shoulders, wincing at the pull on the bandages. "Back to
work, I guess I ought to return this . . ." She fingers the
commando knife. "Maybe later I feel luckier with it on
me." She sheaths it, and pats her old trusty side arm. It feels
better to have a full-sized and fully charged side arm on.
Without speaking, they return to the bridge.

"Status, Mr. Phillips," Emerald demands as they enter.

"Quiet."

"Thank God," she mutters.

There is less clutter here. They cruise along at near top speed, the distance to their objective getting shorter and shorter.

"Sir," the navigation officer calls to the captain, "would you please give us a course bearing?"

"What's up?" Emerald asks, looking at the various data panels.

"We've reached a fork in the road," Dixon says, pointing to the two streams of velvet black which flow out ahead of them.

"Commander Sheller, any orders?" the captain asks formally.

"Beats me," she says under her breath. "Phillips, do we have any data from previous recon missions?"

"No, ma'am. I don't think the Sajo was configured this way when we sent the scouts."

"Great. Just what I needed," she mutters.

"Well, we can always flip a coin," she tells her staff, only half in jest. "It is going to mean time, but we have to send out recon. The problem is that we are getting too damn close to the Marianas fleet to risk any unnecessary intership communication. Send out birds. Fast. I want to know if either or both branches go through or can be punched through. And for God's sake, when the birds are out there, tell them to hurry, but not to get caught."

The birds are launched, one heading for the larger but probably longer and newer stream to the right, the other going for the narrower, but more direct route to the left.

The bird pilot in the narrow passage is traveling at ballistic speeds less than a second from the debris-filled walls of the channel, his on-board computer and luck the only things between him and total destruction. There are places where the "stream" narrows so drastically that he wonders if a cruiser could get through without polishing her hull on the fine debris surrounding him. In some places, chunks of rock and ice as big as his ship zip by so fast they are nothing but a blur.

"Brake, Weasel, brake," his RIO calls on the com.

Weasel pulls up on the stick and wheels back through the space junk, his ship rattling in the chop created by the thousands of tiny impacts.

"That's it, Rabbit, it don't go nowhere," Weasel admits.

"Hey, what if Bluto runs into a wall, too?" Rabbit asks. "How about trying to punch through?"

Weasel is the pilot and has command of his tiny bird. He considers the suggestion and finally decides, "Okay. Let's give it a try, but slow." Even if he was feeling both lucky and courageous, the pilot knows the importance to the mission that he return in one piece and report on the dead end.

After almost half an hour of crawling along in the bone-rattling sandstorm, Rabbit shouts at Weasel, "We're sustaining too much damage. The hull won't hold much longer."

"Going home!" Weasel replies and, disappointed, he turns back to the flotilla.

Hundreds of kilometers away, another bird is also sweeping along, but in a much larger corridor, one that is twisting like a river on a flood plain.

"Any break out there?" the pilot asks her range officer.

"Nothing, Bluto."

"How long have we been doing this, Doc?" she asks her RIO.

"Too long," comes the almost level reply. The RIO knows what his cabinmate is thinking.

"Shit! I'm cranking her up." She pushes the little vehicle to speeds that would make the designing engineer turn gray. "Yahoo!" she belts out, the cry echoed by Doc.

"I have a hole ahead," he yells back.

"That's it! Let's go home," she shouts, rolling the vehicle to a reverse course and nearly scraping the near-solid wall of debris.

On the bridge, Emerald paces between the work stations, looking over the techs' shoulders and generally annoying everyone while waiting for a report.

"Weasel is in hailing range. He says no go. It's a dead end."

It is a full hour more of pacing before she hears from Bluto.

"It's a go!" the pilot's voice crackles over the com.

"Yeah!" A cheer goes up from the entire bridge crew, and Emerald issues the orders for the flotilla to get under way.

The flotilla has lost a total of 1 hour.

If you have run out of time, turn to section 29.

If you have any time left, turn to section 95.

— 95 —

The flotilla reconfigures in a long thin line. In some places, the clear passage is no wider than two ships can safely navigate.

"I hope we don't have any more visitors," Dixon whispers to Phillips, tracing the course with her finger.

"No lie! We'd be sitting ducks! What do we do if we're late?" he asks quietly.

"We join the battle," Dixon whispers back.

They are making good time, and so far they don't seem to have company. But they also are aware of how much their success depends on secrecy.

"We've got a problem ahead."

This announcement makes everybody on the bridge stiffen with fear.

"What is it, radarman?" Captain Hodges demands.

"We've got the mother of all asteroids bearing down on us."

"Show me!"

Sure enough, a huge blip is on a direct collision course with the flotilla.

"Evasive action!" the captain orders.

"No time, sir. It's dead ahead and closing."

"Somebody remind me," Emerald asks. "How are we doing on drones?"

If Emerald still has drones, turn to section 96.

If Emerald has no drones, turn to section 97.

— 96 —

"We've got . . . let me see, operational there are . . ." Phillips sings out the magic number for Commander Sheller. "All armed and ready."

"Launch them on course for the asteroid. No, not to launch rockets, then blow; to kamikaze into it. Order the flotilla to brake. If the drones don't smash it, maybe, just maybe, that'll divert it enough to let us pass."

Each drone is worth an Ordnance Value of 21, but they get only 1 chance apiece. The asteroid requires the equivalent of 2 hits to be destroyed, or a 2 ship kill on your chart.* Total the combat values for the drones you choose to attack with. Roll two six-sided dice once and read the result using Chart D.

If the asteroid is destroyed, turn to section 98.

If not, turn to section 97.

*Total the combat values for the drones you choose to attack with.

— 97 —

"Sorry, ma'am, we are out of drones."
"Conventional fire," Captain Hodges says. "We're going to try to blast it."

You get 2 rolls. The asteroid requires the equivalent of 4 hits between the 2 rounds of fire or a 3 ship kill on one round. Use Chart C.

If the asteroid is destroyed, turn to section 98.

If the asteroid is not destroyed, turn to section 99.

— 98 —

The shock wave rips viciously through the hulls of the ships in the flotilla as the force of the attacks rebounds off the solid rock. Any men not strapped in are thrown from their seats. Seconds later a front of small debris hits the fleet and huge chunks of the asteroid spin dangerously close to several ships. But little real damage is sustained by the already battered ships, and the asteroid is gone.

Another ½ hour has passed; if time has run out, turn to section 29.

If time remains, turn to section 100.

— 99 —

"Damn, it's still on us. Reverse thrust, damn it," Hodges orders.

The huge thing barrels past the *Inverness*, tossing ships to their destruction like a giant bowling ball.

The asteroid attacks once with an Attack Value of 100 on Chart D. If you do not have enough ships to complete the mission, turn to section 29.

If you have survived with enough ships to complete the mission, turn to section 100.

— 100 —

"We are within minutes of our position," Lieutenant Dixon announces.

"Put on some speed. I want to be there early," Emerald says wryly.

"We have a bogey at one o'clock," the radarman breaks in.

"What is it? Break silence. I want a bird on it. What is it?" Emerald shouts.

But she knows what it is. Either her recon bird was spotted when it scouted the passage, or that blown planetoid set off every alarm in the sector, and some smart pirate commander sent out a scout.

"Mother Hen to Chickens. Catch that scout and blast it!

Blast it! I don't care if it's piloted by your grandmother . . . blast it before it can radio back.

"ECM, jam everything, there's no secret something is here. Let's keep 'em guessing what."

Weasel is after the pirate scout like a hawk, with Bluto right behind.

"I have him. I have him. Damn," the pilot roars, his RIO's eyes locked on his instruments. "On him. Steady, steady."

"Move over, Weasel. I've got the speed. Move it, move it," Bluto calls.

"I've got him. I've got him . . ."

Weasel let's a missile fly.

Weasel's Attack Strength is 7 and he fires using Chart C. He gets 1 shot before he is out of range. The scout is unarmed and does not return fire.

If he nails the scout ship, turn to section 101.

If he does not, turn to section 102.

— 101 —

"Got him. Got him. Let's go home!" Weasel shouts.
The two birds swoop back to the flotilla.

Turn to section 103.

— 102 —

"Let me at him," Bluto shouts as she maneuvers past Weasel.

"Steady, steady," Doc intones.

"Locked on target, locked on target. I hope this torp does all it's supposed to."

She lets the missile fly.

Bluto has the enemy targeted with a special tracking missile normally carried only by cruisers. She attacks with an Attack Strength of 7. She fires 1 round from Chart B.

If Bluto destroys the scout, turn to section 101.

If she does not, turn to section 104.

— 103 —

"I want a report from those two bird jocks as soon as they return," Emerald raps out.

Emerald stares at the two faces on the split screen.

"What are our chances that he didn't get a message off before we jammed and you cooked him?"

"Not real good," Bluto offers. "He probably was on-line before we saw him. The big part is they won't know exactly what we have with us. He never got close enough for that."

"I agree with Bluto," Weasel adds.

"Thank you. And, well done."

"Thank you, ma'am," they chorus.

"Well, there goes the ballgame," Emerald sighs. "We'll fight, but they'll know we're coming."

"Just how much difference is that going to make at this point?" the captain asks.

"Probably not much." Emerald blinks at the thought, then shouts, "Oh, of course! Get on a wide broadcast line. Of course! *Inverness* to *Sawfish*, over." She shoves the audio pickup at Captain Hodges, whose face breaks into a grin as he realizes what she is doing.

"*Sawfish* to *Inverness*. This is Captain Hubris speaking," Hodges broadcasts.

Emerald can hardly stifle her laughter as she leans toward the pickup. "I'm sorry, sir, but they have seen us. When we hit them this afternoon, they'll be waiting. We are hurt bad and have no torpedoes or drones left. We can't even reply in code, the comp's out."

"I'm so sorry to hear that, Emerald," the fake Captain Hubris answers. "It means they are onto the fake ships in the gap. I suppose I will just have to hit them with what we have here anyhow and give you a chance to break for home. They can't know how weak we really are or they'd have attacked hours ago. But let's delay by an hour. We'll need time to resupply the guns and tubes.''

The radioman closes the line.

"Do you think they'll buy it?''

"I don't understand,'' Dixon says, looking totally puzzled.

Emerald answers them both. "Simple. Now Hope knows we are ready. He has to know the message was a fake because he is in it. The Marianas fleet can't be sure and with all the ruckus we just kicked up getting here, they had to know something is up.

"If *we* aren't the surprise package, if they think the whole fleet is with us, the main task force will be the surprise. They'll be expecting us, but they will no longer be expecting the attack through the original passage. We have just become the point, and the task force is now the flanking force!''

½ hour was used on the final leg of the run; if there is no time left, turn to section 29.

If there is time left, turn to section 105.

— 104 —

"Break off, break off,'' Mother Hen orders.

"Well, there goes the ball game,'' Emerald sighs. "We'll fight, but they'll know we're coming and in strength.''

"Just how much difference is that going to make at this point?'' the captain asks.

"Probably not much.'' Emerald blinks at the thought, then shouts, "Oh, of course! Get on the wide broadcast line. Of course!''

"*Inverness* to *Sawfish*, over.'' She shoves the audio pickup at Captain Hodges, whose face breaks into a grin as he realizes what she is doing.

"*Sawfish* to *Inverness*. This is Captain Hubris speaking,'' Hodges broadcasts.

Emerald can hardly stifle her laughter as she leans toward the pickup. "I'm sorry, sir, we are down to only three ships and so damaged none of the coding comps are even working. Guess it doesn't matter, not enough of us left to be any help. When we hit them this afternoon, they were waiting.'' She tries to sound tired and frustrated. Tired, she realizes, is easy. If it weren't for the adrenaline raised by the upcoming battle, she'd probably fall over any second.

"I'm sorry to hear that, Emerald," Hodges, as the fake Captain Hubris, answers. "I suppose we will just have to let them go. Your force should exit behind the battle and return home. We will provide a distraction, then disengage ourselves before getting into range. Good luck.''

The radioman closes the line.

"Do you think they'll buy it?''

"I don't understand," Dixon says, looking totally puzzled.

Emerald answers them both. "Simple. They'll be expecting us, but they will no longer be expecting us to attack. Also, if they buy it, Hubris's attack through the original passage will be seen as a distraction. Either way we have added confusion to the enemy. And now Hope knows we are here and ready.

"Now let's go get 'em.''

½ hour was used on the final leg of the run; if there is no time left turn to section 29.

If there is time left, turn to section 105.

— 105 —

Emerald brings her flotilla into position, hidden just within the cover of the space dust and debris. Three small ships hover just inside the cloud, but in detection range. Only those three are allowed to broadcast, and they sing the sad tale of a battered fleet, ready to be destroyed. In the *Inverness* Emerald and the rest sit and wait for the battle to begin. The wait seems like forever, although none of them can ever remember later if they skinned in by minutes or sat there for hours.

Finally they see the *Sawfish* and her escorts charge through the passage, so close on this side, but so long getting to the long way around.

The *Sawfish*'s big guns blaze at the enemy. The Marianas fleet is deployed in a crescent, waiting to trap Emerald's force, hedging in its bet between their original intelligence and the scout's last message followed by Emerald's bogus broadcast. Then the USJ main fleet just keeps on coming through the gap. The pirate fleet turns to face the main task force, momentarily forgetting the threat is the flank. Minutes later Emerald's forces find themselves on the edge of a disordered string of Marianas ships as the whole crescent hurriedly spins to face Hubris. Not a gun faces them as each pirate captain turns his ship to face the most evident threat.

"Okay, folks!" Emerald say triumphantly. "*Now!*"

Congratulations! You have completed your mission, just as Commander Sheller did in Bio of a Space Tyrant: Mercenary.

THE END

If you wish to play again, please return to section 1.

BESTSELLING
Science Fiction
and
Fantasy